Elizabeth Jane Howard was born in March 1923. After training at the London Mask Theatre School she played with a repertory theatre in Devon and at Stratford-on-Avon. During this period she also modelled and worked for the B.B.C. In 1947 she left the theatre to become a secretary. Subsequently she started to review and edit books and to write her own novels. In 1950 she was awarded the John Llewelyn Rhys Memorial Prize for her first book, *The Beautiful Visit*. Her other books include *The Long View*, which was a Book Society choice, *The Sea Change*, *After Julius*, *Something in Disguise*, *Odd Girl Out* and *Getting It Right*, which was the *Yorkshire Post* Novel of the Year for 1982, all of which have been published in Penguins. She has also edited *The Lover's Companion: The Pleasures, Joys and Anguish of Loving*.

Elizabeth Jane Howard

MR WRONG

PENGUIN BOOKS

Penguin Books Ltd, Harmondsworth, Middlesex, England
Penguin Books, 40 West 23rd Street, New York, New York 10010, U.S.A.
Penguin Books Australia Ltd, Ringwood, Victoria, Australia
Penguin Books Canada Ltd, 2801 John Street, Markham, Ontario, Canada L3R 1B4
Penguin Books (N.Z.) Ltd, 182–190 Wairau Road, Auckland 10, New Zealand

—

First published in Great Britain by Jonathan Cape 1975
First published in the United States of America by The Viking Press 1975
Published in Penguin Books 1979
Reprinted 1980, 1983, 1984

—

—

'Toutes Directions' was first published in *Cosmopolitan* in 1973

—

Set, printed and bound in Great Britain by
Cox & Wyman Ltd, Reading
Set in Linotype Georgian

FOR
ELIZABETH TAYLOR

CONTENTS

MR WRONG

EVERYBODY – that is to say the two or three people she knew in London – told Meg that she had been very lucky indeed to find a car barely three years old, in such good condition and at such a price. She believed them gladly, because actually buying the car had been the most nerve-racking experience. Of course she had been told – and many times by her father – that all car dealers were liars and thieves. Indeed, to listen to old Dr Crosbie, you would think that nobody could *ever* buy a second-hand car, possibly even any *new* car, without its brakes or steering giving way the moment you were out of sight of the garage. But her father had always been of a nervous disposition: and as he intensely disliked going anywhere, and had now reached an age where he could fully indulge this disapprobation, it was not necessary to take much notice of him. For at least fifteen of her twenty-seven years Meg silently put up with his saying that there was no place like home, until, certain that she had exhausted all the possibilities of the small market town near where they lived, she had exclaimed, 'That's just it, Father! That's why I want to see somewhere else – *not* like it.'

Her mother, who had all the prosaic anxiety about her only child finding 'a really nice young man, Mr Right' that kind, anxious mothers tend to have – especially if their daughter can be admitted in the small hours to be 'not exactly a beauty' – smiled encouragingly at Meg and said, 'But Humphrey, dear, she will always be coming back to stay. She *knows* this is her home, but all young girls need a change.' (The young part of this had become emphasized as Meg plodded steadily through her twenties with not a romance in sight.)

So Meg had come to London, got a job in an antique shop

in the New King's Road, and shared a two-room flat with two other girls in Fulham. One of them was a secretary, and the other a model: both were younger than Meg and ten times as self-assured; kind to her in an off-hand manner, but never becoming friends, nothing more than people she knew – like Mr Whitehorn, who ran the shop that she worked in. It was her mother who had given Meg three hundred pounds towards a car, as the train fares and subsequent taxis were proving beyond her means. She spent very little in London: she had bought one dress at Laura Ashley, but had no parties to go to in it, and lacked the insouciance to wear it to work. She lived off eggs done in various ways, and quantities of instant coffee – in the shop and in the flat. Her rent was comfortingly modest by present-day standards, she walked to work, smoked very occasionally, and set her own hair. Her father had given her a hundred pounds when she was twenty-one: all of this had been invested, and to it she now added savings from her meagre salary and finally went off to one of London's northern suburbs to answer an advertisement about a second-hand MG.

The car dealer, whom she had imagined as some kind of tiger in a loud checked suit with whisky on his breath, had proved to be more of a wolf in a sheepskin car-coat – particularly when he smiled, which displayed a frightening number of teeth that seemed to stretch back in his raspberry mouth and down his throat with vulpine largesse. He smiled often, and Meg took to not looking at him whenever he began to do it. He took her out on a test drive: at first he drove, explaining all the advantages of the car while he did so, and then he suggested that she take over. This she did, driving very badly, with clashing of gears and stalling the engine in the most embarrassing places. 'I can see you've got the hang of it,' Mr Taunton said. 'It's always difficult driving a completely new car. But you'll find that she's most reliable: will start in all weather, economical on fuel, and needs the minimum of servicing.'

When Meg asked whether the car had ever had an accident, he began to smile, so she did not see his face when he replied that it hadn't been an accident, just a slight brush. 'The respray, which I expect you've noticed, was largely because the panel-work involved, and mind you, it *was* only panel-work, made us feel that it could do with a more cheerful colour. I always think aqua-blue is a nice colour for a ladies' car. And this is definitely a ladies' car.'

She felt his smile receding when she asked how many previous owners the car had had. He replied that it had been for a short time the property of some small firm that had since gone out of business. 'Only driven by one of the directors and his secretary.'

That sounded all right, thought Meg: but she was also thinking that for the price this was easily the best car she could hope for, and somehow, she felt, he knew that she knew she was going to buy it. His last words were: 'I hope you have many miles of motoring before you, madam.' The elongated grin began, and as it was for the last time, she watched him – trying to smile back – as the pointed teeth became steadily more exposed down his cavernous throat. She noticed then that his pale grey eyes very nearly met, but were narrowly saved from this by the bridge of his nose, which was long and thrusting, and almost made up for his having a mouth that had clearly been eaten away by his awful quantity of teeth. They had nothing going for each other beyond her buying and his selling a car.

Back in the showroom office, he sank into his huge moquette chair and said: 'Bring us a coffee, duck. I've earned it.' And a moony-faced blonde in a mini-skirt with huge legs that seemed tortured by her tights, smiled and went.

Meg drove the MG – her *car* – back to London in the first state of elation she had ever known since she had won the bending competition in a local gymkhana. She had a car! Neither Samantha nor Val were in such a position. She really drove quite well, as she had had a temporary job working for a doctor near home who had lost his licence for two years. Away from Mr Taunton (*Clive* Taunton he had repeatedly said), she felt able and assured. The car was easy to drive, and responded, as MGs do, with a kind of husky excitement to speed.

When she reached the flat, Samantha and Val were so impressed that they actually took her out to a Chinese meal with their two boy-friends. Meg got into her Laura Ashley dress and enjoyed every sweet and sour moment of it. Everybody was impressed by her, and this made her prettier. She got slightly drunk on rice wine and lager and went to work the next day, in her car, feeling much more like the sort of person she had expected to feel like in London. Her head ached, but she had something to show for it: one of the men had talked to her several times – asking where she lived and what her job was, and so forth.

Her first drive north was the following Friday. It was cold, a wet and dark night – in January she never finished at the shop in time even to start the journey in the light – and by the time she was out of the rush, through London and on Hendon Way, it was raining hard. She found the turn off to the M1 with no difficulty: only three hours of driving on that and then about twenty minutes home. It was nothing, really; it just seemed rather a long way at this point. She had drunk a cup of strong black instant at Mr Whitehorn's, who had kindly admired the car and also showed her the perfect place to park it every day, and she knew that her mother would be keeping something hot and home-made for her whatever time she got home. (Her father never ate anything after eight o'clock in the evening for fear of indigestion, something from which he had never in his life suffered and attributed entirely to this precaution.)

Traffic was fairly heavy, but it seemed to be more lorries than anything else, and Meg kept on the whole to the middle lane. She soon found, as motorists new to a motorway do, that the lanes, the headlights coming towards her, and the road glistening with rain had a hypnotic effect, as though she and the car had become minute, and she was being spun down some enormous, endless striped ribbon. 'I mustn't go to sleep,' she thought. Ordinary roads had too much going on in them for one to feel like that. About half her time up the motorway, she felt so tired with trying not to feel sleepy that she decided to stop in the next park, open the windows and have a cigarette. It was too wet to get out, but even stopping the windscreen-wipers for a few minutes would make a change. She stopped the engine, opened her window, and before she had time to think about smoking again, fell asleep.

She awoke very suddenly with a feeling of extreme fear. It was not from a dream; she was sitting in the driver's seat, cramped, and with rain blowing in through the open window, but something else was very wrong. A sound – or noises, alarming in themselves, but, in her circumstances, frighteningly out of place. She shut her window except for an inch at the top. This made things worse. What sounded like heavy, laboured, stertorous, even painful breathing was coming, she quickly realized, from the *back* of the car. The moment she switched on the car light and turned round, there was utter silence, as sudden as the noise stopping in the middle of a breath. There was nobody in the back of the car, but the doors were not locked, and her large carrier bag – her luggage – had fallen to the floor. She locked both doors, switched off the car light and the sounds began again, exactly where they had left off – in the middle of a breath. She put both the car light and her headlights on, and looked again in the back. Silence, and it was still empty. She considered making sure that there was nobody parked behind her, but somehow she didn't want to do that. She switched on the engine and started it. Her main feeling was to get away from the place as quickly as possible. But even when she had started to do this and found herself trying to turn the sounds she had heard into something else and accountable, they wouldn't. They remained in her mind, and she could all too clearly recall them, as the heavy breaths of someone either mortally ill, or in pain, or both, coming quite distinctly from the back of the car. She drove home as fast as she could, counting the minutes and the miles to keep her mind quiet.

She reached home – a stone and slate-roofed cottage – at a quarter past nine, and her mother's first exclamation when she saw her daughter was that she looked dreadfully tired. Instantly, Meg began to feel better; it was what her mother had always said if Meg ever did anything for very long away from home. Her father had gone to bed: so she sat eating her supper with surprising hunger, in the kitchen, and telling her mother the week's news about her job and the two girls she shared with and the Chinese-meal party. 'And is the car nice, darling?' her mother asked at length. Meg started to speak, checked herself, and began again. 'Very nice. It was so kind of you to give me all that money for it,' she said.

The week-end passed with almost comforting dullness, and Meg did not begin to dread returning until after lunch on Sunday. She began to say that she ought to pack; her mother said she must have tea before she left, and her father said that he didn't think that *anyone* should drive in the dark. Or, indeed, at all, he overrode them as they both started saying that it was dark by four anyway. Meg eventually decided to have a short sleep after lunch, drink a cup of tea and then start the journey. 'If I eat one of Mummy's teas, I'll pass out in the car,' she said, and as she said 'pass out', she felt an instant, very small, ripple of fear.

Her mother woke her from a dreamless, refreshing sleep at four with a cup of dark, strong Indian tea and two Bourbon biscuits.

'I'm going to pack for you,' she said firmly. She had also unpacked, while Meg was finishing her supper on Friday night. 'I've never known such a hopeless packer. All your clothes were cramped up and crushed together as though someone had been stamping on them. Carrier bags,' she scolded, enjoying every minute; 'I'm lending you this nice little case that Auntie Phil left me.'

Meg lay warmly under the eiderdown in her own room

watching her mother, who quite quickly switched from packing to why didn't Meg drink her tea while it was hot. 'I know your father won't drink anything until it's lukewarm, but thank goodness, you don't take after him. In that respect,' she ended loyally, but Meg knew that her mother missed her, and got tired and bored dealing with her father's ever-increasing regime of what was good or bad for him.

'Can I come next week-end?' she asked. Her mother rushed across the room and enfolded her.

'I should be most upset if you didn't,' she said, trying to make it sound like a joke.

When Meg left, and not until she was out of sight of home, she began to worry about what had happened on the journey up. Perhaps it could have been some kind of freak wind, with the car window open, she thought. Being able even to think that encouraged her. It was only raining in fits and starts on the way back, and the journey passed without incident of any kind. By the time Meg had parked, and slipped quietly into the flat that turned out to be empty – both girls were out – she really began to imagine that she had imagined it. She ate a boiled egg, watched a short feature on Samantha's television about Martinique, and went to bed.

The following week-end was also wet, but foggy as well. At one moment during a tedious day in the shop (where there was either absolutely nothing to do, or an endless chore, like packing china and glass to go abroad), Meg thought of putting off going to her parents but they were not on the telephone, and that meant that they would have to endure a telegram. She thought of her father, and decided against that. He would talk about it for six months, stressing it as an instance of youthful extravagance, reiterating the war that it had made upon his nerves, and the proof it was that she should never have gone to London at all. No – telegrams were out, except in an emergency. She would just have to go – whatever the weather, or anything else.

Friday passed tediously: her job was that of packing up the separate pieces of a pair of giant chandeliers in pieces of old newspaper and listing what she packed. Sometimes she got so bored by this that she even read bits from the old, yellowing newsprint. There were pages in one paper of pictures of a Miss World competition: every girl was in a bathing-dress and high-heeled shoes, smiling that extraordinary smile of glazed triumph. They must have an awfully difficult time, Meg thought – fighting off admirers. She wondered just how difficult that would turn out to be. It would probably get easier with practice.

At half past four, Mr Whitehorn let her go early: he was the kind of man who operated in bursts of absent-minded kindness, and he said that in view of her journey, the sooner she started the better. Meg drank her last cup of instant coffee, and set off.

Her progress through London was slow, but eventually she reached Hendon Way. Here, too, there were long hold-ups as cars queued at signal lights. There were also straggling lines of people trying to get lifts. She drove past a good many of these, feeling her familiar feelings about them, so mixed that they cancelled one another out, and she never, in fact, did anything about the hitchers. Meg was naturally a kind person: this part of her made her feel sorry for the wretched creatures, cold, wet, and probably tired; wondering whether they would *ever* get to where they wanted to be. But her father had always told her never to give lifts, hinting darkly at the gothic horrors that lay in wait for anyone who ever did that. It was not that Meg ever consciously agreed with her father; rather that in all the years of varying warnings, some of his anxiety had brushed off on her – making her shy, unsure of what to do about things, and feeling ashamed of feeling like that. No, she was certainly not going to give anyone a lift.

She drove steadily on through the driving sleet, pretending that the back of her car was full of pieces of priceless chandeliers, and this served her very well until she came to the inevitable hold-up before she reached Hendon, when a strange thing happened.

After moving a few yards forwards between each set of green lights, she finally found herself just having missed yet another lot, but head of the queue in the right-hand lane. There, standing under one of the tall, yellow lights, on an island in the streaming rain, was a girl. There was nothing in the least remarkable about her appearance at first glance: she was short, rather dumpy, wearing what looked like a very thin mackintosh and unsuitable shoes; her head was bare; she wore glasses. She looked wet through, cold and exhausted, but above all there was an air of extreme desolation about her, as though she was hopelessly lost and solitary. Meg found, without having thought at all about it, that she was opening her window and beckoning the girl towards the car. The girl responded – she was only a few yards away – and as she came nearer, Meg noticed two other things about her. The first was that she was astonishingly pale – despite the fact that she had dark, reddish hair and was obviously frozen: her face was actually livid, and when she extended a tentative hand in a gesture that was either seeking reassurance about help, or anticipating the opening of the car door, the collar of her mackintosh moved, and Meg saw that, at the bottom of her white throat, the girl had what looked like the most unfortunate purple birth mark.

'Please get in,' Meg said, and leaned over to open the seat beside her. Then two things happened at once. The girl simply got into the back of the car – Meg heard her open the door and shut it gently, and a man, wearing a large, check overcoat, tinted glasses and a soft black hat tilted over his forehead slid into the seat beside her.

'How kind,' he said, in a reedy, pedagogic voice (almost as though he was practising to be someone else, Meg thought); 'we were wondering whether anyone at all would come to our aid, and it proves that charming young women like yourself behave as they appear. The good Samaritan is invariably feminine these days.'

Meg, who had taken the most instant dislike to him of anyone she had ever met in life, said nothing at all. Then, beginning to feel bad about this, at least from the silent girl's point of view, she asked:

'How far are you going?'

'Ah, now that will surprise you. My secretary and I broke down this morning on our way up, or down to Town,' he sniggered; 'and it is imperative that we present ourselves in the right place at the right time this evening. I only wish to go so far as to pick up our car, which should now be ready.' His breath smelled horribly of stale smoke and peppermints.

'At a garage?' The whole thing sounded to Meg like the most preposterous story.

'Between Northampton and Leicester. I shall easily be able to point the turning out to you.'

Again, Meg said nothing, hoping that this would put a stop to his irritating voice. 'What a bore,' she thought: 'I *would* be lumbered with this lot.' She began to consider the social hazards of giving people lifts. Either they sat in total silence – like the girl in the back – or they talked. At this point he began again.

'It is most courageous of you to have stopped. There are so many hooligans about, that I always say it is most unjust to the older and more respectable people. But it is true that an old friend of mine once gave a lift to a *young man*, and the next thing she knew, the poor dear was in a ditch; no car, a dreadful headache, and no idea where she was. It's perfectly ghastly what some people will do to some people. Have you noticed it? But I imagine you are too young: you are probably in search of *adventure – romance –* or whatever lies behind those euphemisms. Am I right?'

Meg, feeling desperately that *anything* would be better than this talking all the time, said over her shoulder to her obstinately silent passenger in the back: 'Are you warm enough?'

But before anyone else could have said anything, the horrible man said at once: 'Perfectly, thank you. Physically speaking, I am not subject to great sensitivity about temperature.' When he turned to her, as he always seemed to do, at the end of any passage or remark, the smell of his breath seemed to fill the car. It was not simply smoke and peppermints – underneath that was a smell like rotting mushrooms. 'She must be asleep,' Meg thought, almost resentfully – after all there was no escape for *her* – *she* could not sleep, was forced to drive and drive and listen to this revolting front-seat passenger.

'Plastic,' he continued ruminatively (as though she had even *mentioned* the stuff), 'the only real use that plastic has been to society was when the remains, but unmistakable – unlike the unfortunate lady – when the remains of Mrs Durand Deacon's red plastic handbag were discovered in the tank full of acid. Poor Haigh must have thought he was perfectly safe with acid, but of course, he had not reckoned on the durable properties of some plastics. That was the end of *him*. Are you familiar with the case at all?'

'I'm not very interested in murder, I'm afraid.'

'Ah – but fear and murder go hand in hand,' he said at once, and, she felt, deliberately misunderstanding her. She had made the mistake of apologizing for her lack of interest –

'... in fact, it would be difficult to think of any murder where there had not been a modicum, and sometimes, let's face it, a very great deal of fear.' Glancing at him, she saw that his face, an unhealthy colour, or perhaps that was the headlights of oncoming cars, was sweating. It could not still be rain: the car heater was on: it was sweat.

She stuck it out until they were well on the way up the M1. His conversation was both nasty and repetitive, or rather, given that he was determined to talk about fear and murder, he displayed a startling knowledge of different and horrible cases. Eventually, he asked suddenly whether she would stop for him, 'a need of nature', he was sure she would understand what he meant. Just there a lorry was parked on the shoulder, and he protested that he would rather go on –

he was easily embarrassed and preferred complete privacy. Grimly, Meg parked.

'That will do perfectly well,' she said as firmly as she could, but her voice came out trembling with strain.

The man slid out of the car with the same reptilian action she had noticed when he got in. He did not reply. The moment that he was out, Meg said to the girl: 'Look here, if he's hitching lifts with you, I do think you might help a bit with the conversation.'

There was no reply. Meg, turning to the back, began almost angrily: 'I don't care if you are asleep –' but then she had to stop because a small scream seemed to have risen in her throat to check her.

The back seat was empty.

Meg immediately looked to see whether the girl could have fallen off the back seat on to the floor. She hadn't. Meg switched on the car light; the empty black mock-leather seat glistened with emptiness. For a split second, Meg thought she might be going mad. Her first sight of the girl, standing under a lamp on the island at Hendon, recurred sharply. The pale, thin mac, the pallor, the feeling that she was so desolate that Meg had *had* to stop for her. But she had *got into* the car – of course she had! Then she must have got out, when the man got out. But he hadn't shut his door, and there had been no noise from the back. She looked at the back doors. They were both unlocked. She put out her hand to touch the seat: it was perfectly dry, and that poor girl had been so soaked when she had got in – *had got in* – she was certain of it, that if she had *just* got out, the seat would have been at least damp. Meg could hear her heart thudding now, and for a moment, until he returned, she was almost glad that even that man was some sort of company in this situation.

He seemed to take his time about getting back into the car: she saw him – as she put it – slithering out of the dark towards her, but then he seemed to hesitate; he disappeared from sight, and it was only when she saw him by the light of her right-hand side light that she realized he had been walking round the car. *Strolling* about, as though she was simply a chauffeur to him! She called through the window to him to hurry up, and almost before he had got into the car, she said, 'What on earth's become of your secretary?'

There was a slight pause, then he turned to her: 'My *sec*retary?' His face was impassive to the point of offensiveness, but she noticed that he was sweating again.

'You know,' she said impatiently; she had started the engine and was pulling away from the shoulder: 'The girl you said you'd had a breakdown with on your way to London.'

'Ah yes: poor little Muriel. I had quite forgotten her. I imagine her stuffing herself with family high tea and, I don't doubt, boy-friend – some provincial hairdresser who looks like a pop star, or perhaps some footballer who looks like a hairdresser.'

'What *do* you mean?'

He sniggered. 'I am not given to oversight into the affairs of any employee I may indulge in. I do not like prolonged relationships of any kind. I like them sudden – short – and sweet. In fact, I – '

'No – *listen!* You know perfectly well what I'm talking about.'

She felt him stiffen, become still with wariness. Then, quite unexpectedly, he asked: 'How long have you had this car?'

'Oh – a week or so. Don't make things up about your secretary. It was her I really stopped for. I didn't even see you.'

It must be his sweat that was making the car smell so much worse. 'Of course, I noticed at once that it was an MG,' he said.

'The girl in the back,' Meg said desperately: he seemed to be deliberately stupid as well as nasty. 'She was standing on the island, under a lamp. She wore a mac, but she was obviously soaked to the skin, I beckoned to her, and she came up and got into the back without a word. At the same time as you. So come off it, inventing nasty, sneering lies about your secretary. Don't pretend *you* didn't know she was there. You probably used her as a decoy – to get a lift at all.'

There was a short, very unpleasant silence. Meg was just beginning to be frightened, when he said, 'What did your friend look like?'

It was no use quibbling with him about not being the girl's friend. Meg said: 'I told you ...' and instantly realized that she had done nothing of the kind. Perhaps the girl really hadn't been his secretary ...

'All you have done is allege that you picked up my secretary with me.'

'All right. Well, she was short – she wore a pale mac – I told you that – and, and glasses – her hair was a dark reddish colour – I suppose darker because she was wet through, and she had some silly shoes on and she looked *ill*, she was so white – a sort of livid white, and when she –'

'Never heard of her – never heard of anyone like her.'

'No, but you *saw* her, didn't you? I'm sorry if I thought she was your secretary – the point is you saw her, didn't you? *Didn't* you?'

He began fumbling in his overcoat pocket, from which he eventually drew out a battered packet of sweets, the kind where each sweet is separately wrapped. He was so long getting a sweet out of the packet and then starting to peel off the sticky paper that she couldn't wait.

'Another thing. When she put out her arm to open the door, I saw her throat –'

His fingers stopped unwrapping the paper. She glanced at them: he had huge, ugly hands that looked the wrong scale beside the small sweet –

'She had a large sort of birth mark at the bottom of her throat, poor thing.'

He dropped the sweet: bent forward in the car to find it. When, at last, he had done so, he put it straight into his mouth without attempting to get any more paper off.

Briefly, the smell of peppermint dominated the other, less pleasant odours. Meg said, 'Of course, I don't suppose for a moment you could have seen *that*.'

Finally, he said: 'I cannot imagine who, or what, you are talking about. I didn't see any *girl* in the back of *your* car.'

'But there couldn't be someone in the back of my car without my knowing!'

There seemed to Meg to be something wrong about his behaviour. Not just that it was unpleasant; wrong in a different way; she felt that he knew perfectly well about the girl, but wouldn't admit it – to frighten her, she supposed.

'Do you mind if I smoke?'

He seemed to be very bad at lighting it. Two matches wavered out in his shaky hands before he got an evil-smelling fag going.

Meg, because she still felt a mixture of terror and confusion about what had or had not happened, decided to try being very reasonable with him.

'When you got into the car,' she began carefully, 'you kept saying "we" and talking about your secretary. *That's* why I thought she must be.'

'Must be what?'

A mechanical response; sort of playing-for-time stuff, Meg thought.

'You must excuse me, but I really don't know what you are talking about.'

'Well, I think you *do*. And before you can say "do what?" I mean *do* know what you are talking about.'

She felt, rather than saw him glance sharply at her, but she kept her eyes on the road.

Then he seemed to make up his mind. 'I have a suggestion to make. Supposing we stop at the next service area and you tell me all about everything? You have clearly got a great deal on your mind; in fact, you show distinct symptoms of being upset. Perhaps if we –'

'No thank you.' The idea of his being the slightest use to talk to was both nauseating and absurd. She heard him suck in his breath through his teeth with a small hissing sound: once more she found him reminding her of a snake. Meg hated snakes.

Then he began to fumble about again, to produce a torch and to ask for a map. After some ruminating aloud as to where they were, and indeed where his garage was likely to be, he suggested stopping again 'to give my, I fear, sadly weakened eyes an opportunity to discover my garage'.

Something woke up in Meg, an early warning or premonition of more, and different trouble. Garages were not marked on her map. She increased their speed, stayed in the middle lane until a service station that she had noticed marked earlier at half a mile away loomed and glittered in the wet darkness. She drove straight in and said:

'I don't like you very much. I'd rather you got out now.' Again she heard him suck his breath in through his teeth. The attendant had seen the car, and was slowly getting into his anorak to come out to them.

'How cruel!' he said, but she sensed his anger. 'What a pity! What a chance lost!'

'Please get out at once, or I'll get the man to turn you out.' With his usual agility, he opened the door at once, and slithered out.

'I'm sorry,' Meg said weakly: 'I'm sure you did know about the girl. I just don't trust you.'

He poked his head in through the window. 'I'm far from sure that I trust you.' There were little bits of scum at the ends of his mouth. 'I really feel that you oughtn't to drive alone if you are subject to such extreme hallucinations.'

There was no mistaking the malice in his voice, and just as Meg was going to have one last go at his admitting that he had seen the girl, the petrol attendant finally reached her and began unscrewing her petrol cap. He went, then. Simply withdrew his head, as though there were not more of him than that, and disappeared.

'How many?'

'Just two, please.'

When the man went off slowly to get change, Meg wanted to cry. Instead, she locked all the doors and wound up the passenger window. She had an unreasonable fear that he would come back and that the attendant might not help her to oust him. She even forgot the change, and wound up her own window, so that nobody could get into the car. This made the attendant tap on her window; she started violently, which set her shivering.

'Did you – did you see where the man who was in the front of my car went? He got out just now.'

'I didn't see anyone. Anyone at all.'

'Oh thank you.'

'Night.' He went thankfully back to his brightly lit and doubtless scorching booth.

Before she drove off, Meg looked once more at the back seat. There was no one there. The whole experience had been so prolonged, as well as unnerving, that apart from feeling frightened she felt confused. She wanted badly to get away as fast as possible, and she wanted to keep quite still and try to sort things out. He *had* known that the girl had been in the car. He had enjoyed – her fear. Why else would he have said 'we' so much? This made her more frightened, and her mind suddenly changed sides.

The girl *could not* have got out of the back without opening and shutting – however quietly – the door. There had been no sound or sounds like that. In fact, from the moment the girl had got into the car she had made no sound at all. Perhaps she, too, had been frightened by the horrible man. Perhaps she had *pretended* to get in, and at the last moment, slipped out again.

She opened her window wide to get rid of the smells in the car. As she did so, a possible implication of what the petrol attendant had said occurred. He hadn't seen *anyone*; he hadn't emphasized it like that, but he had repeated 'anyone at all'. Had he just meant that he hadn't looked? Or had he looked, and seen nobody? Ghosts don't talk, she reminded herself, and at once was back to the utterly silent girl.

Her first journey north in the car, and the awful breathing sounds coming from its back, could no longer be pushed out of her mind. The moment that she realized this, both journeys pounced forward into incomprehensible close-ups of disconnected pictures and sounds, recurring more and more rapidly, but in different sequences, as though, through their speed and volume, they were trying to force her to understand them. In the end, she actually cried out: 'All *right*! The car is haunted. Of course, I see that!'

A sudden calm descended upon her, and in order to further it, or at least stop it as suddenly stopping, she added: 'I'll think about it when I get home,' and drove mindlessly the rest of the way. If any spasm about what had recently happened attempted to invade her essential blankness, she concentrated upon seeing her mother's face, smelling the dinner in the kitchen, and hearing her father call out who was there.

'. . . thought he might be getting a severe cold, so he's off to bed. He's had his arrowroot with a spot of whisky in it and asked us to be extra quiet in *case* he gets a wink of sleep.'

Meg hugged her without replying: it was no good trying to be conspiratorial with her mother about her father; there could never be a wink or a smile. Her mother's loyalty had stiffened over the years, until now she could relate the most absurd details of her father's imaginary fears and ailments with a good-natured but completely impassive air. 'Have we got anything to drink?' she asked.

'Darling – I'm sure we have somewhere. But it's so unlike you to want a drink that I didn't put it out. It'll be in the corner cupboard in the sitting-room.'

Meg knew this, knew also that she would find the untouched half-bottles of gin and Bristol Milk that were kept in case anyone 'popped in'. But the very few people who did always came for cups of tea or coffee at the appropriate times of day. Her parents could not really afford drink – except for her father's medicinal whisky.

When she brought the bottles into the kitchen, she said, 'You have one too. I shall feel depraved drinking all by myself.'

'Well dear, then I'll be depraved with you. Just a drop of sherry. We needn't tell Father. It might start him worrying about your London Life. Been meeting anyone interesting lately?'

Meg had offered her mother a cigarette with her sherry, and her mother, delighted, had nearly burned her wispy fringe bending over the match to light it, and was now blowing out frantic streams of smoke from her nose before it got too far. It was all right to smoke if you didn't inhale. On a social occasion, that was. Like it being all right to drink a glass of sherry at those times.

'This *is* nice,' her mother said, and then added, 'Have you been *meeting* anyone nice, dear? At all your parties and things?'

It was then that Meg realized that she could not possibly – ever – pour out all her anxieties to her mother. Her mother simply would not be able to understand them. 'Not this week,' she said. Her mother sighed, but Meg was not meant to hear, and said that she supposed it took time in a place like London to know people.

Meg had a second, strong gin, and then said that she would pay her mother back, but she was tired, and needed a couple of drinks. She also smoked four cigarettes before dinner, and felt so revived that she was able to eat the delicious steak-and-kidney pie followed by baked apples with raisins in them. Her mother had been making Meg Viyella nightgowns with white lace ruffles, and wanted to show them to her. They were brought into the kitchen, which was used for almost everything in winter as it saved fuel. 'I've been quite excited about them,' her mother said, when she laid out the nightgowns. 'Not quite finished, but such fun doing each one in a different colour.'

She listened avidly when Meg told her things about Mr Whitehorn and the shop: she even liked being told about the *things* in the shop. She laughed at Meg's descriptions when they were meant to be in the least amusing, and looked extremely earnest and anxious when Meg told her about the fragility and value of the chandeliers. When it was time to go to bed, and she had filled their two hot-water bottles, she accompanied Meg to the door of her bedroom. They kissed, and her mother said: 'Bless you, dearie. I don't know what I'd do without you. Although, of course, one of these days I shall have to when Mr Right comes along.'

Meg cleaned her teeth in the ferociously cold bathroom and went back to her – nearly as cold – bedroom. Hot-water bottles were essential: Viyella nightdresses would be an extra comfort. From years of practice, she undressed fast and ingeniously, so that at no time was she ever naked. Whenever her mother mentioned Mr Right she had a vision of a man with moustaches and wearing a bowler hat mowing a lawn. She said her prayers kneeling beside her high, rather uncomfortable bed, and the hot-water bottle was like a reward.

In the night she awoke once, her body tense and crowded with fears: 'I could *sell* the car, and get another,' she said, and almost at once relaxed, the fears receded until they fell through some blank slot at the back of her mind and she was again asleep.

This decision, combined with a week-end of comfortingly the same ordered, dull events made her able to set aside, almost to shut up, the things – as she called them – that had happened, or seemed to have happened, in the car. On Sunday morning she found her mother packing the back with some everlasting flowers 'for your flat', a huge, dark old tartan car-rug 'in case you haven't enough on your bed', and a pottery jar full of home-made marmalade 'to share with your friends at breakfast'.

'There's plenty of room for the things on the floor, as you're so small, really, that you have your driving seat pushed right forward.'

When she said good-bye and set off, it was with the expec-

tation of the journey to London being uneventful, and it
was.

The trouble, she discovered, after trying in her spare time
for a week, was that she *could not* sell the car. She had
started with the original dealer who had sold it to her, but he
had said, with a bland lack of regret, that he was extremely
sorry, but this was not the time of year to sell second-hand
cars and that the best he could offer was to take it back for a
hundred pounds less than she had paid for it. As this would
completely rule out having any other car excepting a
smashed-up or clapped-out Mini that would land her with
all kinds of garage bills (and, like most car-owners, Meg was
not mechanically minded), she had to give up that idea from
the start.

She advertised in her local newspaper shop (cheap, and it
would be easy for people to try out the car) but this only got
her one reply: a middle-aged lady with a middle-aged poodle
who came round one evening. At first it seemed hopeful; the
lady said it was a nice colour and looked in good condition,
but when she got into the driver's seat with Meg beside her
to drive it round the block, her dog absolutely refused to get
into the back as he was told to do. His owner tried coaxing,
and he whimpered and scrabbled out of the still-open door;
she tried a very unconvincing authority: 'Cherry! Do as you
are told at once,' and his whimpering turned to a series of
squealing yelps. 'He *loves* going in cars. I don't know what's
come over him!'

Out in the street again, all three of them, he growled and
tried to snap at Meg. 'I'm sorry dear, but I can't possibly buy
a car that Cherry won't go in. He's all I've got. Naughty
Cherry. He's usually such a mild, sweet dog. Don't you dare
bite at Mummy's friends.'

And that was that. She asked Mr Whitehorn and her flat-
mates, and finally, their friends, but nobody seemed to want
to buy her car, or even wanted to help her get rid of it. By
Friday, Meg was in a panic at the prospect of driving north

again in it. She had promised herself that she wasn't going
to, and as long as the promise had seemed to hold (surely she
could find *someone* who would want it) she had been able
not to think about the alternative. By Friday morning she
was so terrified that she did actually send a telegram to her
mother, saying that she had 'flu and couldn't drive home.

After she had sent it, she felt guilty and relieved in about
equal proportions. The only way she could justify such behaviour was to make sure of selling the car that week-end.
Samantha told her to put in an ad in the *Standard* for the
next day. 'You're bound to make the last edition anyway,'
she said. So Meg rang them, having spent an arduous half-
hour trying to phrase the advertisement. 'Pale blue MG – '
was how it finally began.

Then she had to go to work. Mr Whitehorn was in one of
his states. It was not rude to think this, since he frequently
referred to them. There was a huge order to be sent to New
York that would require, he thought, at least a week's packing. He had got hold of tea chests, only to be told that he
had to have proper packing cases. There was plenty of newspaper and straw in the basement. He was afraid that that
was where Meg would have to spend her day.

The basement was whitewashed and usually contained
only inferior pieces, or things that needed repair. While
working, Meg was allowed to have an oil stove, but it was
considered too dangerous to leave it on by itself. Her first job
was a huge breakfast, lunch, tea and coffee service bought by
Mr Whitehorn in a particularly successful summer sale in
Suffolk. It had to be packed and listed, all two hundred and
thirty-six pieces of it. It was lying on an old billiard table
with a cut cloth, and Meg found that the most comfortable
way to pack it was to bring each piece to a chaise-longue
whose stuffing was bristling out at every point, and put the
heap of newspapers on the floor beside her. Thus she could
sit and pack, and after each section of the set she could put
things back on the table in separate clutches with their
appropriate labels. She was feeling much better than when

she had woken up. Not having to face the drive: having put an advertisement into a serious paper almost made her feel that she had sold the car already: Val had said that she might go to a film with her on Sunday afternoon if her friend didn't turn up and she didn't think he would, so that was something to look forward to, and packing china wasn't really too bad if you took it methodically and didn't expect ever to finish.

In the middle of the morning, Mr Whitehorn went out in his van to fetch the packing cases. He would be back in about an hour, he said. Meg, who had run up to the shop to hear what he said – the basement was incredibly muffled and quiet – made herself a mug of coffee and went back to work. There was a bell under the door-rug, so that she could hear it if customers came.

She was just finishing the breakfast cups when she saw it. The newspaper had gone yellow at the edges, but inside, where all the print and pictures were, it was almost as good as new. For a second, she did not pick up the page, simply stared at a large photograph of head and shoulders, and MI MYSTERY in bold type above it.

The picture was of the girl she had picked up in Hendon. She knew that it was, before she picked it up, but she still had to do that. She *might* be wrong, but she knew she wasn't. The glasses, the hair, the rather high forehead ... but she was smiling faintly in the picture ...

'... petite, auburn-haired Mary Carmichael was found wrapped in her raincoat in a ditch in a lane not one hundred yards from the MI north of Towcester. She had been assaulted and strangled with a lime green silk scarf that she was seen wearing when she left her office ... Mr Turner was discovered in the boot of the car – a black MG that police found abandoned in a car-park. The car belonged to Mr Turner, who had been stabbed a number of times and is thought to have died earlier than Miss Carmichael ...' –

She realized then that she was reading a story continued from page one. Page one of the newspaper was missing. She

would never know what Mr Turner looked like. She looked
again at the picture of the girl. 'Taken on holiday the previous year.' Even though she was smiling, or trying to smile,
Mary Carmichael looked timid and vulnerable.

'. . . Mr Turner, a travelling salesman and owner of the car,
is thought to have given a lift or lifts to Mary Carmichael
and some other person, probably a man, not yet identified.
The police are making extensive inquiries along the entire
length of the route that Mr Turner regularly travelled. Mr
Turner was married, with three children. Miss Carmichael's
parents, Mr and Mrs Gerald Carmichael of Manchester,
described their only daughter as very quiet and shy and
without a boy-friend.'

The paper was dated March of the previous spring.

Meg found that her eyes were full of tears. Poor, poor
Mary. Last year she had been an ordinary timid, not very
attractive girl who had been given a lift, and then been horribly murdered. How frightened she must have been before
she died – with being – assaulted – and all that. And now,
she was simply a desolate ghost, bound to go on trying to get
lifts, or to be helped, or perhaps even to *warn* people . . . 'I'll
pray for you,' she said to the picture, which now was so blur-
red through her tears that the smile, or attempt at one,
seemed to have vanished.

She did not know how long it was before the implications,
both practical and sinister, crept into her mind. But they did,
and she realized that they had, because she began to shiver
violently – in spite of feeling quite warm – and fright was
prickling her spine up to the back of her neck.

Mystery Murders. If Mr Turner was not the murderer of
Mary, then only one other person could be responsible. The
horrible man. The way he had talked of almost nothing but
awful murders . . . She must go to the police immediately.
She could describe him down to the last detail: his clothes,
his voice, his tinted spectacles, his frightful smell . . . He had
been furious with her when she had put him down at the
service station . . . but, one minute, before that, before *then*,

when she had let him out on the shoulder where the lorry was, he had taken ages to come back into the car – had walked right round it, and then, when he got in, and she had questioned him about the girl, and described her, he had become all sweaty, and taken ages to reply to anything she said. He must have *recognized* the car! She was beginning to feel confused: there was too much to think about at once. This was where being clever would be such a help, she thought.

She began to try to think quietly, logically: absolutely nothing but lurid fragments came to mind: 'a modicum, and sometimes, let's face it, a very great deal of fear'; the girl's face as she stood under the light on the island. Meg looked back at the paper, but there was really no doubt at all. The girl in the paper *was* the same girl. So – at last she had begun to sort things out – the girl *was* a ghost: the car, therefore, must be haunted. He certainly knew, or realized, something about all this: his final words – 'I'm far from sure that *I* trust *you*' – that was because she had said that she didn't trust him. So – perhaps he thought she *knew* what had happened. Perhaps he had thought she was trying to trap him, or something like that. If he *really* thought that, and he was actually guilty, he surely wouldn't leave it at that, would he? He'd be afraid of her going to the police, of what, in fact, she was shortly going to do. He couldn't *know* that she hadn't seen the girl before, in the newspaper. But if he couldn't know, how could the police?

At this point, the door-bell rang sharply, and Meg jumped. Before she could do more than leap to her feet, Mr Whitehorn's faded, kindly voice called down. 'I'm back, my dear girl. Any customers while I've been away?'

'No.' Meg ran up the stairs with relief that it was he. 'Would you like some coffee?'

'Splendid notion.' He was taking off his teddy-bear overcoat and rubbing his dry, white hands before the fan heater.

Later, when they were both nursing steaming mugs, she asked: 'Mr Whitehorn, do you remember a mystery murder case on the M1 last spring? Well, two murders, really? The man was found in the boot of the car, and the girl – '

'In a ditch somewhere? Yes, indeed. All over the papers. The real trouble is, that although I adore reading detective stories, *real* detective stories. I mean, I always find real-life crime just dull. Nasty, and dull.'

'I expect you're right.'

'They caught the chap though, didn't they? I expect he's sitting in some tremendously kind prison for about eighteen months. Be out next year, I shouldn't wonder. The law seems to regard property as far more important than murder, in my opinion.'

'Who did they catch?'

'The murderer, dear, the murderer. Can't remember his name. Something like Arkwright or James. Something like that. But there's no doubt at all that they caught him. The trial was all over the papers, as well. How have you been getting on with your marathon?'

Meg found herself blushing: she explained that she had been rather idle for the last half hour or so, and suggested that she make up the time by staying later. No, no, said Mr Whitehorn, such honesty should be rewarded. But, he added, before she had time to thank him, if she *did* have an hour to spend tomorrow, Saturday morning, he would be most grateful. Meg had to agree to this, but arranged to come early and leave early, because of her advertisement.

The worst of having had that apparently comforting talk with Mr Whitehorn was that if they *had* already caught the man, then there couldn't be any point in going to the police. She had no proof that she hadn't seen a picture of poor Mary Carmichael; in fact, she realized that she might easily have done so, and simply not remembered because she didn't read murder cases. Going to the police and saying that you had seen a ghost, given a ghost a *lift* in your car, and *then* seen a picture in a newspaper that identified them, would just sound hysterical or mad. And there would be no point in describing the horrible man, if, in fact, he was just horrible but not a murderer. But at least she didn't have to worry about him: his behaviour had simply seemed odd and then sinister, *before* Mr Whitehorn had said that they had caught the murderer. There was nothing she needed to do about any of it. Except get rid of a haunted car.

After her scrambled eggs and Mars bar, she did some washing, including her hair and her hair-brush, and went to bed early. Just before she went to sleep, the thought occurred to her that her mother always thought that people – all people – were really better than they seemed, and her father was certain that they were worse. Possibly, they were just *what* they seemed – no more and no less.

In the morning, second post, she got a letter from her mother full of anxiety and advice. The letter, after many kind and impractical admonitions, ended: 'and you are not to think of getting up or trying to drive all this way unless you are feeling completely recovered. I do wish I could come down and look after you, but your father thinks he may be getting this wretched bug. He has read in the paper that it is all over the place, and is usually the first to get anything, as you know. Much love, darling, and take *care* of yourself.'

This made Meg feel awful about going to Mr Whitehorn's but she had promised him, and letting down one person gave one no excuse whatsoever for letting down another. Samantha had promised to sit on the telephone while Meg was out, as she was waiting for one of her friends to call.

When she got back to the flat, Samantha was on the telephone, and Val was obviously cross with her. 'She's been *ages* talking to Bruce and she is going out with him in a minute, and I said I'd do the shopping, but she won't even say what she wants. She's a drag.'

Samantha said: 'Hold on a minute – six grapefruit and two rump steaks – that's all,' and went on listening, laughing and talking to Bruce. Meg gazed at her in dismay. How on earth were people who had read her advertisement and were *longing* to ring her up about it to get through? The trouble about Samantha was that she was so *very* marvellous to look at that it was awfully difficult to get her to do anything she didn't want to do.

Val turned kindly to Meg and said loudly: 'And your ad's in, isn't it? Samantha – you really are the limit. Meg, what would you like me to shop for you?'

Meg felt that this was terribly kind of Val, who was also pretty stunning, but in a less romantic way. Neither of the girls had ever shopped for her before; perhaps Val was going to become her friend. When she had made her list of cheese, apples, milk, eggs and Nescaff, Val said, 'Look, why don't we share a small chicken? I'll buy most of it, if you'll do the cooking. For Sunday,' she added, and Meg felt that Val was almost her friend already.

Val went, and at once, Samantha said to the telephone: 'All *right*: meet you in half an hour. Bye.' In one graceful movement she was off the battered sofa and stood running her hands through her long, black hair and saying: 'I haven't got a *thing* to wear!'

'Did anyone ring for me?'

'What? Oh – yes, one person – no, two, as a matter of fact. I told them you'd be in by lunch-time.'

'Did they sound interested in the car?'

'One did. Kept asking awful technical questions I couldn't answer. The other one just wanted to know if the car could be seen at this address and the name of the owner.' She was pulling off a threadbare kimono, looking at her face in a small, magnifying mirror she seemed always to have with her. 'Another one ...! They keep bobbing up like corks! I've gone on to this diet not a moment too soon.'

An hour went slowly by: nobody rang up about the car. Samantha finally appeared in fantastically expensive-looking clothes as though she was about to be photographed. She borrowed 50p off Meg for a taxi and went, leaving an aura of chestnut bath-stuff all over the flat.

The week-end was a fearful anti-climax. On Saturday, three people rang up – none of them people who had called before; one said that he thought it was a drop-head, seemed,

indeed, almost to accuse her of it not being, although she
had distinctly said saloon in her ad. Two said they would
come and look at the car: one of these actually arrived, but
he only offered her a hundred pounds less than she was
asking, and that was that. On Sunday morning Meg cooked
for ages, the chicken and all the bits, like bread sauce and
gravy, that were to live up to it. At twelve-thirty Val got a
call from one of her friends, and said she was frightfully
sorry, but that she had to be out to lunch after all.

'Oh dear! Shall I keep it till the evening? The chicken will
be cold, but the other –'

Val interrupted her by saying with slight embarrassment
that she wouldn't be back to dinner, either. '*You* eat it,' she
ended, with guilty generosity.

When she had gone, the flat seemed very empty. Meg
tried to comfort herself with the thought that anyway, she
couldn't have gone to the cinema with Val, as she would
have to stay in the flat in case the telephone rang. But she
had been looking forward to lunch. If a person sat down to a
table with you and had a meal, you stood a much better
chance of getting to know them. Sundays only seemed
quieter in London than they were in the country, because of
the contrast of London during the week. As she sat down to
her leg of chicken with bread sauce, gravy and potatoes done
as her mother did them at home, she wondered whether
coming to London was really much good after all. She did
not seem to be making much headway: it wasn't turning out
at all how she had imagined it might, and at this moment
she felt rather homesick. Whatever happened, she'd go home
next week-end, and talk to her mother about the whole
thing. Not – the car – thing, but Careers and Life.

Two more people rang during the afternoon. One was for
Samantha, but the other was about the car. They asked her
whether she would drive it to Richmond for them to see it,
but when she explained why she couldn't they lost interest.
She kept telling herself that it was too long a chance to risk
losing other possible buyers by going out for such a long

time, but as the grey afternoon settled drearily to the darker grey evening, she wondered whether she had been wrong.

She wrote a long letter to her mother, describing Samantha's clothes and Val's kindness, and saying that she was already feeling better (another lie, but how could she help it?): then she read last month's *Vogue* magazine and wondered what all the people in it, who wore rich car-coats and gave fabulous, unsimple dinner-parties and shooting lunches and seemed to know at least eight ways of doing their hair, were doing now. On the whole, they all seemed in her mind to be lying on velvet or leather sofas with one of their children in a party dress sitting quietly reading, and pots of azaleas and cyclamen round them in a room where you could only see one corner of a family portrait and a large white or honey-coloured dog at their feet on an old French carpet. She read her horoscope: it said, you will encounter some interesting people, but do not go more than half-way to meet them, and watch finances – last month's horoscope anyway, so that somehow whether it had been right or not hardly counted. When she thought it must be too late for any more people to ring up, she had a long, hot bath, and tried to do her hair at least one other way. But her hair was too short, too fine, and altogether too unused to any out-landish intention, and obstinately slipped or fell back into its ordinary state. It was also the kind of uninteresting colour that people never even bothered to describe in books. She yawned, a tear came out of one eye, and she decided that she had better get on with improving her mind, to which end she settled down to a vast and heavy book on Morocco that Val said people were talking about . . .

All week she packed and packed: china, glass, silver and bits of lamps and chandeliers. On Wednesday, someone rang up for her at the shop while she was out buying sausage rolls and apples for Mr Whitehorn's and her lunches. Mr White-horn seemed very vague about them: it hadn't seemed to be about the car, but something about her week-end plans, he thought. He *thought*, he reiterated, as though this made the whole thing more doubtful. Meg could not think who it could be – unless it was the very shy young man with red hair and a stammer who had once come in to buy a painting on glass about Nelson's death. He had been very nice, she thought, and he had stayed for quite a long time after he had bought the picture and told her about his collection of what she had learned to call Nelsoniana. That was about the only person it could be, and she hoped he'd ring again, but he didn't.

By Wednesday, she had long given up hope of anyone buying the car as a result of the advertisement. Val and Samantha told her that Bruce and Alan both said it was the wrong time of the year to sell second-hand cars, and she decided that she had better try to sell it in the north, nearer home.

On Wednesday evening she had a sudden, irrational attack of fear. However much she reasoned with herself, she simply did not *want* to drive up the M1 alone in the car that she was now certain was haunted. She couldn't stand the thought of hearing the sounds she had heard, of seeing the girl again in the same place (possibly, why not? – ghosts were well known for repeating themselves): and when Samantha and Val came in earlier than usual and together, she had a – possibly not hopeless – idea. Would either or both of them like to come home for the week-end with her?

Their faces turned at once to each other; it was easy to see the identical appalled blankness with which they received the proposal. Before they could *say* that they wouldn't come, Meg intercepted them. 'It's lovely country, and my mother's a marvellous cook. We could go for drives in the car – ' but she knew it was no good. They couldn't possibly come, they both said almost at once: they had dates, plans, it was awfully kind of her, and perhaps in the summer they might – yes, in the summer, it might be marvellous *if* there was a free week-end ...

Afterwards, Meg sat on her bed in the very small room

that she had to herself, and cried. They weren't enough her friends for her to plead with them, and if she told them why she was frightened, they would be more put off than ever.

Next morning she asked Mr Whitehorn if he had ever been up north to sales and auctions and things like that.

Yes, he went from time to time.

'I suppose you wouldn't like to come up this week-end to stay? I could drive you to any places you wanted to go.'

Mr Whitehorn looked at her with his usual tired face, but also with what she could see was utter amazement.

'My dear child,' he said, when he had had time to think of it, 'I couldn't possibly do anything, *anything* at all like that at such short notice. It would throw out all my plans, you see. I always make plans for the week-end. Perhaps you have not realized it,' he went on, 'but I am a homosexual, you see. I thought you would know; running this shop and the states I get into. But I *always* plan my free time. I am lunching with a very dear friend in Ascot, and sometimes, not always, I stay the night there.' The confidence turned him pink. 'I had absolutely no intention of *misleading* you.'

Meg said of course not, and then they both apologized to each other and said it didn't matter in the least.

On Thursday evening both girls were out, and Meg, who had not slept at all well for the last two nights, decided that she was too tired to go on her own to the cinema, although it was *A Man for All Seasons* that she had missed and always wanted to see. She ate a poached egg and half a grapefruit that Samantha said was left over from her diet, and suddenly she had a brain-wave. What she was frightened of, she told herself, was the idea that the poor girl would be waiting for her again at Hendon. If, therefore, she *avoided* Hendon, and got on to the M1 further north, she would be free of this anxiety. There might still be those awful sounds again, like she had heard the first time, but she would just have to face that, drive steadily home, and when she got there, she decided, she would jolly well tell her mother about the whole thing. The idea, and the decision to tell her mother, cheered her so much that she felt less tired, and went down to the car to fetch the map. There, the car rug that her mother had given her in case she did not have enough on her bed pricked her conscience. She had managed to toil up the stairs with the flowers and marmalade and her case, but she had completely forgotten the rug; this was probably because her mother had put it in the car herself, and it now lay on the floor in the back. She would take it home, as she really didn't need it, and usually her father used it to protect his legs from draughts when he sat in or out of doors.

She found a good way on the map. She simply did not go left on to Hendon Way, but used the A1000 through Barnet and turned left on to the St Albans road. She could get on to the M1 on the way to Watford. It was easy. That evening she packed her party dress so that her mother could see it. She always packed the night before, so that she didn't rush too much in the mornings, got to work on time, and parked her car, as usual, round the corner from the shop. Mr Whitehorn had simply chalked 'No Parking' on the brick wall, and so far it had always worked.

On Friday morning, she and Mr Whitehorn met each other elaborately, as though far more had occurred between them than had actually happened: the first half hour was heavy with off-handed good will, and they seemed to get in each other's way far more often than usual. They used the weather as a kind of demilitarized zone of conversation. Mr Whitehorn said that he heard on the wireless that there was going to be fog again, and Meg, who had heard it too, said oh dear and thanked him for telling her. Later in the morning, when things had eased between them, Mr Whitehorn asked her whether she had been successful in selling her car. Trains were so much easier in this weather, he added. They were, indeed. But she could hardly tell him that as she lived seventeen miles from the station, and her parents didn't drive, and the last bus had left by the time the train she would be able to catch had arrived, and her salary certainly couldn't afford a taxi . . . she couldn't tell him any of that: it would look like asking, begging for more money – she would never do it . . .

But the train became a recurrent temptation throughout the long cold and, by the afternoon, foggy day. She banished the idea in the end by reminding herself that, with the cost of the advertisement, she simply did not have the money for the train fare: the train was out of the question.

Mr Whitehorn, who had spent the morning typing lists for the Customs (he typed with three fingers in erratic, irritable bursts), said that he would buy their lunch, as he needed the exercise.

When he had gone, Meg, who had been addressing labels to be stuck on to the packing cases, felt so cold that she fetched the other paraffin heater from the basement and lit it upstairs. She did not like to get another cardigan from her case in the car, as in spite of its being so near, it was out of sight from the shop, and Mr Whitehorn hated the shop to be left empty for a moment. This made her worry, stupidly, whether she had locked the car. It was the kind of worry that one had like wondering if one had actually posted a letter *into* the letter-box: of course, one would have, but once any idea to the contrary set in, it would not go. So the moment he came back with hot sausages and Smith's crisps from the pub, she rushed out to the car. She had, in fact, left one back door open: she could have sworn that she hadn't, but there it was. She got herself another cardigan out of her case in the boot, and returned to her lunch. It was horrible out; almost dark, or at any rate opaque, with the fog, and the bitter, acrid air that seemed to accompany fogs in towns. At home, it would be a thick white mist – well, nearly white, but certainly not smelling as this fog smelled. The shop, in contrast, seemed quite cosy. One or two people came to 'look around' while they ate; but there was never very much to see. Mr Whitehorn put all the rubbish that got included in lots he had bid for on to trays with a mark saying that anything on the tray cost 50p, or £1. Their serious stuff nearly always seemed to go abroad, or to another dealer. Mr Whitehorn always made weak but kindly little jokes about his rubbish collectors, as he called the ones who bought old photograph albums, moulded glass vases, or hair-combs made of tortoise-shell and bits of broken paste.

While she was making their coffee, Meg wondered whether perhaps Mr Whitehorn would be a good person to talk about the haunted car to. Obviously, asking him to stay had been a silly mistake. But he might be just the person to understand what was worrying her; to believe her and to let her talk about it. That was what she most wanted, she realized. Someone, almost anyone, to *talk* to her about it: to sort out what was honestly frightening, and what she had imagined or invented as fright.

But immediately after lunch, he set about his typing again, and got more and more peevish, crumpling up bits of paper and throwing them just outside the waste-paper basket, until she hardly liked to ask him, at five, whether she might go.

However, she did ask, and he said it would be all right.

He could not know how difficult she found it to leave: she said good night to him twice by mistake, started to put her old tweed coat on, and then decided that with the second cardigan she wouldn't need it, took ages tying on her blue silk head-square, and nearly forgot her bag. She took out her car keys while she could find them easily in the light, shut the shop door behind her and, after one more look at him, angrily crouched over his typewriter, went to the car.

Once she got into the car, her courage and common sense returned. It was only, at the worst, a four-hour journey: she would be home then, and everything would be all right. She flung her overcoat into the back – it was far easier to drive without it hanging round the gear lever – had one final look at her map before she shut the car door, and set off.

It was more interesting going a different way out of London, even though it seemed to be slower, but the traffic, the fog, and making sure all the time that she was on the right road, occupied her mind, almost to the exclusion of anything else. She found her way on to the M1 quite easily; the signs posting it were more frequent and bigger than any other sign.

She drove for over an hour on the motorway, and there was no sound in the car, no agonized, laboured breathing – nothing. It was getting rather hot, but the heater cleared the windscreen and she couldn't do without it for long. The fog was better, too, although patchy, and in the clearer bits she could see the fine misty rain that was falling all the time. She was sticking to the left-hand lane, because although it meant that lorries passed her from time to time, she felt safer in the fog than if she had been in the middle, and possibly unable to see either side of the road. She opened a crack of window because the car seemed to be getting impossibly hot and full of stale air. Another two hours, she thought, and decided that she might as well stop to take off her thick cardigan – she could use the hard shoulder just for that – and perhaps she had made far too much of her nerves and anxiety about the whole journey. She drew up carefully, and then saw a service area ahead – safer in one of those. 'At least I didn't give in,' she thought, and thought also how ashamed of herself she would have been if she had.

As she drew up in the car-park, she was just about to get out of her cardigan, when a huge hand reached out in front of her and twitched the driving mirror so that she could see him. He was smiling, his eyes full of triumph and malice. His breath reeked over her shoulder as she gave a convulsive gasp of pure shock. 'You must be a ghost!' She heard herself repeating this in a high voice utterly unlike her own. 'You must be a ghost: you *must* be!'

'Only had to pick the car lock twice. You shouldn't have locked it *again* in the middle of the day.'

She knew she should start the car and drive back out on to the road, but she couldn't see behind her, and nearly lost all control when she felt something hard and pointed sticking into the back of her neck.

'They caught Mr Wrong, you see. But you seemed to know

so much, and as you were driving the same car, I simply had to catch up with you somehow. Two birds with one stone, as it were.'

She made an attempt to get the brake off, but a hand clamped over her wrist with such sudden force that she cried out.

'Ever since you turned me out in that unkind manner, I have been trying to track you down. That is all I have done, but your advertisement was a great help.' She saw him watching her face in the mirror and licking the scum off his lips. She made a last effort.

'I shall turn you out again – any minute – I shall!'

He sucked in his breath, but he was still smiling.

'Oh no, you won't. This time, it will all be done my way.'

She thought she screamed once, in that single second of astonished disbelief and denial before she felt the knife jab smoothly through the skin on her neck when speechless terror overwhelmed her and she became nothing but fear – heart thudding, risen in her throat as though it would burst from her: she put one hand to the wound and felt no knife – only her own blood – there, as he said:

'Don't worry *too* much: just stick to fear. The fate worse than death tends to occur after it. I've always liked them warm.'

SUMMER PICNIC

THE illusion that eating in the open air constitutes at least one aspect of the simple life is ancient and enduring, but now, if the contents of all three cars were unloaded on to the lawn and somebody who didn't know about the picnic was asked what it was all for, they might equally have thought that it was the blitz, or a bazaar, or the result of some mysterious crisis like the *Mary Celeste*. Apart from immense quantities of provisions, the parents and their friends took rugs and mackintoshes, dark glasses, cameras and alcohol, cigarettes, writing paper and newspapers, a trug and a trowel for moss-collecting (they were going to a wood), an air cushion and a collapsible bath-chair, and a huge umbrella like a vulture which opened inside or out with impartial difficulty. The nannies took shopping baskets filled with white emergency baby equipment and slow constructive things like knitting. The children (divided roughly into two groups) took a tent, electric torches, books whose lives hung on a single linen thread, butterfly nets, pen-knives that would either never open or never shut, wine gums, a few ravenous caterpillars in a biscuit tin, a bottle filled with sea water and marked POYSIN, and a very battered game of Monopoly. The younger children and the babies took some string, a bunch of dandelion heads, and the number of stuffed animals that their nannies thought good for them. The dogs were not allowed to bring anything.

Lalage, who had not had to prepare either children or food, who was not responsible for the weather or for the motor-cars, who had, in fact, arrived at the perfect picnic age of seventeen, had spent two delicious hours hovering between a white dress and a yellow: brushing her yellow hair, polishing her Spanish sandals, and painting her nails; telling herself continually that she must remain calm, perfectly calm, and that it could not possibly rain, at least not before they had all met everybody from the other house.

Now she wandered restlessly from room to room watching the car being methodically packed by one of her parents, and as methodically disarranged and re-packed by the other: waiting for the exact moment to appear when she would neither be subjected to torturing minutes of heat in an immobile car, nor squeezed in unmercifully because she had been forgotten ... but she felt they would be hours yet. The rooms already had that empty sunlit air, when a blue-bottle or even a butterfly trapped between the sashes of the windows seemed to make an enormous noise, and heavy petals fell momentously on to tables of mahogany and satin-wood, exposing the charming freckled hearts of mid-summer roses ...

Lalage's mother edged her back cautiously against the tree which she had chosen rather because it commanded the scene than afforded her comfort, and extracted a drowning insect from her cider. Her chief anxieties were over: food was unpacked; banks of sandwiches were being demolished; little pools of salt and of lemonade lay on the groundsheets; hard-boiled eggs and leaves of cos lettuce winked and wilted on the elegant turf. Nannies were manoeuvring the significant contents of sandwiches into the petulant and in-discriminate mouths of their charges; and the children – Lalage's mother glanced at the little sunbaked clearing where they had elected to picnic, shuddered, and thought very hard about Andrew Marvell's restoring poem.

Lalage, on the other hand, lay on a mossy bank of dark delicious green, with her hands clasped behind her golden head, while that nice young man who drove too fast peeled her a nectarine, and told her about motor-cars. Suddenly, Lalage's mother remembered reclining in a punt on the Thames (oh the agony with one's corsets until one had ad-justed the seat either bolt upright, or almost flat) in her best white flannel skirt and poplin blouse, and her boater tipped over her eyes in a way that Mamma had condemned as unbecoming, while another nice young man had broken off an enthusiastic monologue about horses to stammer that she was so splendid to talk to, and might he, could he, could he possibly call her Lillian? He had only enjoyed the delectable advantage for one afternoon: Lillian's Mamma had hurriedly sent her to Scotland, where she was expected to fly as high as the grouse and marry a peer. But she had married a commoner, and her Mamma had acquiesced (after all there were five daughters and no means). Mamma was now possibly asleep. The fact that she sat upright in her bath-chair meant nothing. She had lunched off cold turtle soup and Bath Oliver biscuits, and was now immobile; reeking gently of white violets, and with her diamond rings glaring on her cold, freckled fingers – she was always cold . . . Her eyes were shut.

The young man leapt to his feet, held out a hand to Lalage, and pulled her up beside him. The sudden ease of the impulse made them both smile faintly at one another, as they stood for a moment before strolling away down one of the bridle-paths. Lillian glanced apprehensively at her Mamma, and then at the children, who appeared to be on the brink of a quarrel, which, considering the conditions in which they were picnicking, was hardly surprising. They had pitched a dark brown tent on a baked cart-track. Inside, swathed in car-rugs, they were eating, and playing Monopoly, a game which its perpetrators would barely have recognized – so personal and complex had it become. Occasionally, a younger child would be sent for reinforcements of food. It was sweating so profusely, and so incapacitated by its car-rug, that it was hopelessly inefficient. Lillian had suggested to one of them that they might like to explore the wood, but it had looked at her with purple streaming contempt, and hobbled away. At frequent intervals the tent collapsed upon its occupants and any incipient quarrel was shelved while they feverishly restored their airless gloom.

One of the babies began to cry. He had lunched lightly off dandelion heads, some milk chocolate, and a Monopoly card, and was now quite properly resisting any further nourishment. He was hurried away into the wood by a nurse, but not, Lillian feared, before he had had ample opportunity to waken Mamma ...

Lalage's grandmother, however, was awake, although since lunch she had successfully persuaded everybody to the contrary. In reality her mind had played upon the scene before her and receded into the past, very much as the chequered streaking sunlight trembled and shifted over the leaves on their branches on the trees, and apparently back into the woods. So she reflected upon the people she could see, and more that she could remember; upon present and past picnics, and the unchanging behaviour of picnickers – pretending the moment they arrived in some romantic or beautiful place that they were in fact at home, only in houses without furniture, which made them either somnolent and dull, or grumpy and restless. The men were almost all asleep, and the women were clearing the debris of the meal. In her young days – sixty-odd years ago – one had really eaten luncheon in the open air. Picnic food had been properly exotic; had by no means degenerated to the mere sandwich. She remembered very young broad beans cooked and frozen in their butter; little tailor-made cold roast birds; delicious claret cup; elaborate galantine; cold *soufflés*; an entire Stilton; trifle such as those poor children in the tent had never seen; and quantities of fruit the perfection of which seemed mysteriously to have vanished today – with the handsome man and good dinner-table conversation. It was better now to be very old, or the age of that granddaughter escaping into the woods to discover whether she liked being kissed.

She remembered doing exactly the same thing on a picnic, only then it was far more difficult, and consequently exciting; and afterwards telling her younger, plainer, sister (Oh Laura! How could you? Oh Laura!): and she remembered that she had been far more excited at telling about it than at the event itself. She had had to escape from the party with its perimeter of servants and ponies, and stroll away up the glen path picking wood anemones which were certain to die even before they reached the carriages which awaited their return down on the road. She had walked, and picked her anemones, until she could no longer hear the party but only the cool frenzied rush of the stream pouring down the glen, below her path. Then the effort of carrying her flowers and her parasol had seemed too great, and she had selected a clean grey boulder in the shade on which to settle carefully. She had hovered for hours that morning between a white frock and a yellow, and had chosen the white muslin as more becoming; but already her skirts were marked with green round the hem from bruised bluebell leaves.

He had surprised her exactly when she had expected him; and she had confirmed her imagination of his kissing her to the accompaniment of a hectic streaking kingfisher, and the faint seductive smell of wild garlic. Their promises had seemed as endless as the golden silver stream: but the following week he had been sent to India with his regiment; and she had never heard what became of him. She had married a gentle impoverished baronet ... And here was Lalage returned with her young man; both in an elaborate state of flushed indifference ...

In the car going home, Lalage's grandmother suddenly gave her an immense diamond ring.

Lalage held the hand that wore the ring with the hand that didn't for the rest of the journey, and wondered whether any picnic could be more perfect than this picnic, which had, in fact, altered her whole life, only nobody would understand that, any more than they remembered or understood that she was now seventeen ...

Lillian, driving another car home – not too fast because it was overloaded, but fast enough to allow the child who was always sick in cars to be sick at home for a change, wondered in an exhausted manner why people described anything difficult or nerve-racking as 'no picnic'.

Lalage's grandmother, after giving away her ring, settled to pretending to be asleep; reflecting sadly on the sad and lonely thought that there was nobody left alive to stare at the ringless finger and say, 'Oh Laura! How could you? Oh Laura!'

'WELL, here we are anyway,' Alan said as he edged the Rover into a meagre slot of the car-park.

Nobody answered him. Ruth, his wife, was so exhausted by having tried to prevent an embarrassing row in front of the girls – their sixteen-year-old daughter and a friend – that she literally couldn't think of anything to say. Julie didn't want to prolong any of the interminable grown-up talk that seemed to accompany the slightest grown-up plan, and Christine, the friend, was examining with her compact mirror something on her cheekbone that was either a mosquito bite or worse, possibly a spot of some kind.

They got slowly out of the car. It was intensely hot, and the tall trees that edged one side of the park were so dusty that they were hardly green at all. Throngs of people in holiday clothes, dark glasses and irrelevant hats wandered to and fro from the cars, the tourist stall placed under a bluff of the rocky cliff by the road, and the road to the river. The moment that they were all out of the car, they started to separate: the girls gravitated to the stall where hideous wares were constantly stared at and fingered, but seemed hardly ever to be bought. Ruth looked beyond the trees at the place below – like a large village square laid out with trees and tables for picnickers, and wondered whether they could buy wine for their meal. Alan was struggling with the boot of the car that went on being difficult to open whatever the garage did to it. 'Streuth! *Christ!*' he was screaming inside. He looked round. Of course they had all gone off and left him to it: as usual. One of the things you'd expect with a woman you were – whom you weren't in love with any more – was that they should be *practical*. Even more practical and reliable than you'd thought of them as being when you *were* in love with them. But Ruth seemed to have got worse. Sometimes she almost behaved as though she was *bored* with him! It was a bit much when he was making such an effort not to feel that about her. 'Ruth!' he called, as heartily as he could. 'The boot's open! Ruth!'

Christine had bought herself a white stetson hat at the tourist stall. In it, she contrived to look both dashing and demure. Instantly Julie had wanted one, but when she put it on, she looked like a schoolgirl in a fancy-dress hat. 'I look so *healthy*!' she wailed – trying to make a joke from her disappointment. Her friend merely looked at her and in a voice of damning neutral frankness, said: 'Your calves are too thick.' 'I know.' She didn't even look down at them. 'Better when they're brown, though.' 'Mm.' 'She might at least agree with that,' Julie thought sadly. Her parents were gesticulating.

'Your mother thinks we should have lunch, and I think we should have a bathe.'

'I didn't say we should have lunch *now*; I meant we should go and see whether we can buy bread and wine and so on by the picnicking place, because if we can't we'll have to drive somewhere to get it before we bathe.'

'Why – "before we bathe"?'

'Alan, you *know* why. Because all French shops shut for the afternoon.'

'French shops!' he repeated derisively – as though she had invented them to be a nuisance. He turned to the boot of the car. 'Right! Let us defer our bathe. Let us repack the boot. It won't take all that long if we all help.'

'Daddy, surely we needn't repack the boot just to see if they sell food?'

'Now which are we to do? Are we going to have lunch and then bathe, are we going to pack up the boot or not? I simply want to know. I don't care in the least *what* we bloody well do if only you'd make up your minds.' His face, scalded by sun, was also steaming from sweat; his sparse, pale ginger hair had gathered into sodden spiky strands, his dry white forearms were blooming with yellow freckles. He was far too hot, Ruth thought: he insisted on spending his holidays in the heat, and it really didn't suit him.

'I'll go and find out,' she said, and ran to the steps down on to the picnic place. But when she returned to tell him that all was well; they could buy anything they needed to supplement their meal, she found them still standing paralysed round the boot of the car, Alan in that attitude of exaggerated patience that had always depressed her.

'We still don't know whether you want to unpack *every*-thing, or simply the bathing things.'

'Alan, for goodness' sake! Of course we don't want to take all the picnic to the bathing place. *Ob*viously we don't!'

He straightened up from trying either to wedge or unwedge a basket from the boot. 'Obviously? Obviously?'

Ruth turned to the girls. 'Why don't you go on, you two? Down there and there's some steps down to the river-bank just before the bridge.'

'O.K.' They trailed off, wandering slowly rather than walking, in a way that made them look as though they were going to bump into everyone else. When she thought they had got far enough, she said:

'Let's go and have a cool drink before we join them.'

He shut the boot after two irritable attempts without replying, and Ruth, who could now hear her own heart beating, repeated: 'Why not have a quick one? The children will be perfectly happy now they can bathe.'

'If you've *quite* made up your mind,' he began savagely, but she interrupted.

'Alan, I've had all I can stand this morning. If you're determined to have a row, at least let's have it on our own. It's not fair on Julie.'

They walked without speaking along the car-park and down the steps to the picnic square. Here were small iron tables and battered chairs, and by the steps a large booth selling much what any French grocery shop sells – fruit, bread, drink, *pâtés* and cheeses.

'I'd like a beer,' Ruth said before that could become a point of argument.

'Go and sit down then.' He went to the booth and began to wait with ostentatious patience while a French family bought their lunch.

Ruth lit a cigarette. Her hands were shaking.

Julie and Christine eventually reached the rocks at the edge of the river. They had not spoken during their short, hot walk there; Christine did not usually start conversations, and Julie, who admired her deeply, felt too much ashamed of her parents to know what to say. Loyalty fought with her embarrassment – after all, everyone knew that parents were a drag in some way or other: it just seemed extraordinary the way hers could turn what was meant to be a nice, easy, normal day into something cross and complicated. They argued about everything, which was the same as nothing; and even when they weren't actually rowing, they seemed unable to *do* anything without endless discussion. She supposed it was their age – or ages – Mummy was five years younger than Dad, but when you got as old as they were, five years wouldn't seem much. Anyway, even she seemed too old to enjoy anything. 'Past it,' she thought sadly. 'Going to try the water,' she muttered to her friend, but Christine seemed not to hear her.

There was a good shelf of rock at the very edge and sheer below it, so that one could sit and put one's legs in the river, which was now the light greeny brown of unreliable eyes. Below were crowds of little, dull, silver fish darting aimlessly about. Above, and high on the left, hung the Pont du Gard – giant, honey-coloured arches crammed with sky like blue cream. The people on top walking through the aqueduct looked tiny, and their voices seemed louder than their size. The water felt unexpectedly cool. 'I won't swim yet,' she thought, and got up to join her friend, saying, 'I do want to walk right across the top, don't you?'

'Not especially. I mean, what would be special about it?'

'Oh – I don't know.' What she meant was that she did know, but felt embarrassed about explaining. To walk on stones put there by the Romans – to imagine the water coursing through and try to imagine how deep it must have been, to look down on the wooded gorge with its pebbly shoals and its deep pools and to think that it must always have looked the same – since the Romans, anyway – seemed worth doing and something that one would always remember, but of course, if people didn't feel like that, you couldn't make them. Anyway, Christine was probably a bit upset by the awful parking scene.

'I'm sorry about when we got here.'

'That's all right. You couldn't help it.'

'You can't imagine how awful it is to have your parents still married to each other.'

Christine didn't answer, and Julie looked anxiously to see why. She had taken off her jeans, and now wore the briefest brown bikini and her stetson. Her feet were bare, her toenails painted white: she was rubbing oil into her long, wand-like legs, that seemed all skin and narrow bones. Lucky, lucky her.

'It simply means they don't have to try. Whereas, if they'd both started again with someone else, they'd all be terrifically friendly out of guilt. Do you think it's Change of Life?'

Christine took a glass out of her Greek bag and examined her face. 'Just their age, I expect. After all, they haven't got much to look forward to.' She felt and prodded the spot. 'I don't think old people have any emotional depths. At that age, their whole lives are ruled by boring things like money and comfort. I don't mean just your parents,' she added generously, 'I should think it's just general lack of sex.'

'It must be.' Julie felt that it was most likely that her parents' mysterious but boring malaise should be due to something equally mysterious – although not boring, of course. Sex was part of some brave state she passionately aspired to – prevented, she sometimes felt, by the shape of her legs, but in her more optimistic moments feeling that it might just be a matter of stopping being sixteen. Christine was seventeen and a half, and in love with her English teacher at school. He was also in love with her, but married, and Christine was frightfully brave about it. Christine knew a terrific amount about sex and her view of marriage was simple and damning. 'It's just a way of not having to worry any more,' she had said at school ... Julie had become her confidante last term as her older friend had left. This meant that she could tell Julie everything she wanted to tell, with Julie being in no position to counter-attack. Nothing whatever had happened to Julie; even her elder sister getting married earlier this summer had been written off by Christine as a bourgeois happening. Julie hadn't discovered whether her sister and Simon had had any sex before marriage, and after that, Christine simply hadn't wanted to know. 'Mortgage on a house,' she had scoffed, when Julie had produced this as adult earnest of their intentions. 'Nothing to do with real love. Just a cart before the horse.' Julie had felt snubbed, which had taken the form of making her wonder – with a sudden, but very convincing fear – whether she might never *grow up*; simply stay in this outside inferior state with nobody falling in love with her for years and years – her heart breaking, her virginity intact ... She was jolly well not going to let Christine get into the mood to snub her now. 'Have you heard from Jasper?' she asked respectfully.

Christine's face softened to self-interest and she started burrowing in the Greek bag. 'A fabulous letter,' she began.

It wasn't difficult to keep her in a good temper.

'Can I have a cigarette – quickly – before they come?'

'Yeah. I can't read you all of it, of course. But his wife has found out.' She had produced the bulky letter in its flimsy envelope.

'Of course you can't. I understand that,' said Julie.

To begin with Ruth watched Alan trying to get the beer,

but when two German tourists had eased – if that was the word for it – their way in front of him at the counter, she gave up; tried to relax before the storm. Because now, she felt, she would have to tell him. It seemed to her then that for years she had been seeking excuses to avoid a showdown, as much as she had sought to appease her guilt. The last excuse (and it ought to be the last) had been their elder daughter's marriage. Margaret, bless her heart, had always been so average a child in every way (not bad-looking, not unintelligent, not absolutely without a sense of humour), that Ruth was irrationally confounded when she returned from Leeds with another student who looked, in jeans, gold-rimmed glasses and long, dry, brown hair so much like her that her mother had thought they might be taken for sisters until he turned out not only to be a man, but her future son-in-law. Margaret's wedding had to be gone through with the utmost convention: any hint of a rift between her parents would have upset Margaret; she was training to be a social worker like Simon, and already felt that the upper-middle classes had no right to emotional upheaval. But that was over.

Then there had been the question – *was* being – of Julie's summer holiday. At sixteen she still needed the family set-up. A friend from school completed her idea of a good time, but she was not yet old enough to want to go and stay away on her own. So here they were. Alan had chosen the place; she couldn't imagine why he always imagined that he liked heat when every year it made him come out in rashes and bumps and get so cross . . .

Alan at last brought their beers to the table, but then announced that he was going to find a gents. His bringing the beer forced her to get back to her problem – was it a crisis, or not? She simply could not go on living with him in this angry and sterile atmosphere of pointless, cheerless fault-finding and argument. It was obvious that he was unhappy too, and with the children nearly finished, surely she could come clean, tell him everything and get the hell out? For a moment she imagined the getting out, but before she was beyond her first picture of it – Mervyn's face when she told him that at last she was free – Alan had returned.

'I've been thinking,' he said, in tones of one to whom the practice was unfamiliar. 'I feel I ought to – look, I've been feeling so awful, you see – the least I can do is explain a bit ...'

'Oh God,' she thought; 'he's ill! He's got some ghastly illness he's been trying to face by himself!' She took another cigarette and handed the packet to him; her hands, she noticed, had started to shake again.

'I've been having this affair, you see. I expect you knew, really, there didn't seem any point in actually telling you ...'

She didn't say that there had been so many affairs that she no longer distinguished between one and another. He had only once told her about a girl, after it was over, and then he had made it painfully plain that Melanie had been the one (and only) love of his life. He had been too distraught then for her to bring up the previous occasions. It was before she had even met Mervyn, and she had thought her own world was coming to an end. After that, she had slipped slowly and painlessly out of love with him ...

'... for months I didn't notice her – well, I thought she was a nice girl – jolly good secretary and all that – until one day I came into my office and found her crying – some bloody bastard had let her down ...'

Mervyn's lined and craggy face with eyes both brilliant and kind beneath amazing eyebrows rose up before her – annihilating any impatience, any cruelty – however oblique –with her husband and his Everyman saga. Mervyn never thought ill of people, and anyway, was not one of those boring men who said all he thought.

'... started by us just having a drink after work: she led an awful cramped little life at home with her parents – she's never had anyone to talk to before ... Anyone decent, I mean,' he added with a self-deprecating laugh.

And I used to sit at home wondering whether to have the

casserole with Julie after her homework, or whether to put it back in the oven and wait.

'. . . an only child; which always makes that kind of sterile, suburban life worse . . .'

You get only wives too. They don't have other wives to moan at or gossip with. They have to be alone all day, and all evening too, if their only husband doesn't come home. You can't talk to children; they have to be protected. There's a case for saying that being an only child is a jolly good preparation for being a wife.

'. . . short of it was that we fell in love. I told her that I was married,' he added, implying that this showed that he had done all that could be expected of him. 'She was marvellous about it. She said she didn't mind. That a little of me was much better than none at all.'

I bet she did. But Mervyn wasn't married, so shut up. He was waiting for her. He'd waited eight years now, and had said then, and still said, that he'd wait until she felt free to come to him. I am too lucky to be a bitch. Poor Alan. But if he feels like this why can't I go? Just take Julie, and go?

'. . . it *would* be just before this holiday, she suddenly seemed different. I mean, by then we'd – oh well, you remember that last week-end you had to go to Westmorland on that research job?'

Indeed yes. Mervyn, though never demanding, had proved a virtuoso at designing reasons that for years now had enabled them to be together 'enough to keep us kicking', he said.

'Well, I took her to Amsterdam. We had a fantastic time. Sorry – I don't want to hurt your feelings,' he went on, as though they had just occurred to him. 'You know how it is.'

'Yes,' she said, before she could stop herself.

'You really *are* imaginative about other people – in a good kind of way. But don't worry.' He laughed bitterly. 'You haven't lost your husband. She's gone off. Some boring little yob she met on the Costa Brava *last year*. When I asked her, last year, whether she'd enjoyed herself, she just said the place was fabulous, but she'd missed me. She never said a word about him. I knew something was wrong about a month ago, but she was so sensitive, she didn't want to tell me. I forced it out of her in the end. She just couldn't stand our situation. I see it's an awful one for a woman – feeling that whatever a man feels about it he's got his life elsewhere; that she can never be more than a sort of fringe part of his life. So there it is. It's all over. She was married exactly three weeks and two days after Margaret. I'm glad I told you, really. I've been feeling so lousy. You see, I don't know whether she hasn't resorted to marriage just to get away from me. I asked her and all she would say was that she and Lionel had a lot in common. She was being tactful – loyal – about him. I quite see that. I quite see that if she was going to marry him, she had to, you know, *stand* by him.'

'Yes,' Ruth said – it being the safest if not the only thing to say.

'You agree? You probably know much better than I how a woman's mind works – even if you aren't familiar with the circumstances. Anyway, she's left the office. There it is. Here I am, as it were.' He tried to laugh; it clearly hurt him.

'Poor Alan.' Her remarks, she thought, were like the exit signs from a motorway; inevitable, evenly spaced, designed for safety.

Again he tried to laugh. 'The thing is – what I *can't* convey – is, well, I was in love with her, that's all. I'm *still* in love with her. She's so *young*, you see. Life seems utterly meaningless: the thought of it going on and on and on ...' He buried his head in his large, freckled hands for a moment, and when he took them away, she saw that his eyes were full of tears.

'Time will make it easier in the end.' A cliché had always to be offered tentatively to be accepted, she had discovered.

'That's what they all say, isn't it?' He blew his nose, and then took one of her cigarettes. As she lit it for him, she said:

'Perhaps it's better to have had a little of something that was good, rather than nothing at all.'

He looked sharply at her, to see whether there was anything of self-pity or autobiography behind this suggestion, but her face was blank of anything but proper concern. He looked – of course without knowing it – so like a large dog that had been suddenly and savagely kicked.

'Yes,' he said, but in his own case entirely disagreeing with her: 'I know.'

'I've got you, though, haven't I?' he said. 'I mean – a lot of people – well – not a lot, but people who get into this situation, often haven't anyone – have to face it alone. I'm lucky, really, aren't I? I mean, *you'll* always be there. We've been together – what is it – twenty-something years now. It's a long time when you come to think of it.'

'A very long time.' She got to her feet. 'Do you think perhaps that we should join the girls now?'

'Good old Ruth.' He put his hands painfully on her sunburned shoulder.

While they walked, as briskly as the heat would allow, down the dusty road and the steps to the river, she thought of that week-end in Westmorland – in March it had been – when she and Mervyn had camped in a friend's cottage – slept on a mattress in front of a huge log-fire for comfort, lived on ham, bananas, oatcakes and honey and sardines and Terry's bitter chocolate. She had picked wild daffodils for the first time in her life, and one morning they had climbed to the summit of Scafell where there was still early spring snow on which they had lain to make love. The soft, cold air had carried only the rasping cry of young lambs across great shoulders and valleys of silence. 'I have much more than luck,' she thought. 'I have the only thing that matters: what everybody in the world will pray for, pretend about, emulate and envy. I'm so lucky I can put up with anything: I can wait.'

At the bottom of the steps she turned to him.

'We'll have a lovely refreshing bathe and a delicious picnic.'

He managed a watery smile. 'Good old Ruth,' he said again.

Julie thought her father looked positively *down*-trodden when he joined them. Her mother's face had a calm, almost serene appearance. She had been getting at Daddy, no doubt. Although Daddy was (obviously) frightfully intelligent, there was also something pathetic about him. Christine had said that women sometimes got horrible during the Change of Life. Poor Dad.

'I'll race you, Dad, to the other side,' she said encouragingly. 'It's hardly cold at all, when you're used to it.'

He did not answer at once, and she looked quickly at him to see that he was all right. He was fine – he was only looking at Christine.

Christine lay, looking fabulous, on her towel spread upon the uneven rocks with her Greek bag as a pillow. She had not bathed yet; all the ghastly things she had told Julie from Jasper's letter must have upset her. 'I'd be crying buckets if I was her,' Julie thought. But she had not cried at all, had explained all about how one had to be objective and it was all experience. Now her father was saying:

'I thought I'd like to have a look at the *pont* before a swim. Christine? Would you like to have a go?'

Before Christine could reply, Julie exclaimed:

'I'd love to, Daddy.'

Without looking at her, he said irritably: 'You're wet. I don't want to wait ages while you dry and change.'

Christine had sat up, and was pulling on her jeans. Now she smiled at Daddy.

'I'd simply adore to come,' she said.

After her father and Christine had left, her mother, without a word, handed her a cigarette, and then, after she had lit it, said:

'Let's have our fags and then a swim. *Then* we'll have lunch, and if you feel like it, you and I might go up on the aqueduct. I'd love you to tell me about it.'

Julie, who had felt horribly outside and snubbed, felt tears pricking her eyes again, so she simply nodded. Then she thought that Dad might be more *interesting*, but perhaps Ma was nicer. It must be awful not to have anything exciting to look forward to, and she really couldn't help her age ...

'SHE's ever so natural, as you can see.' Mrs Bracken re-crossed her legs so that Mr Big (as she privately called each film-director she encountered) could see her ankles to better advantage. 'Has simply no idea that she's not like other children.'

They both looked at Mrs Bracken's daughter, who stood at the far end of the huge room, biting her nails with such furtive virtuosity that Ted Strong – the director – wondered whether she had had more years of practice at that (and everything else) than Mrs Bracken claimed.

'Fern! Come over here, dear. Say good morning to Mr – Mr Strong in French.'

'Bonjour.' Fern advanced in tiny steps towards Mr Strong: when she reached him, she curtsied and repeated: 'Bonjour, M'sieur.' She wore red tights and a navy-blue crocheted tunic that suggested a smock. A dwarf pregnant would be the heraldic term. Her flaxen hair flowed down her back, and her patent-leather strap shoes were rounded childishly at the toes. Her ears were pierced and adorned with tiny little golden balls. 'Comment ça va?' she piped. 'No natural, she,' Ted thought wearily, and came back at once to the watchful dragon Mum. He was used to them: he had made commercials for telly and there was a constant need for children.

'She can get along in five languages, can do ballet, tap dance, *or* modern dance. She has appeared since the age of three. She's eight, now, and of course, I've never neglected her education. She photographs quite beautifully, but the agency will have given you the file on her.'

There was a silence during which Ted tried to think how to get rid of Mrs Bracken in order to find out what Fern might be like without her, and Mrs Bracken wondered feverishly what to make Fern do that would catch the director's interest. Fern stood with her hands behind her back staring at her shoes and hating their rounded toes. Outside, huge slanting snowflakes floated down against the window.

'Fern was a snowflake once – in a panto scene in ever such a big film. Fern, do you remember that little song you used to sing when you did that nice little routine and wore that pretty white and silver tutu?'

Fern looked at her, and Ted looked at Fern, thereby missing the ferocious, but secret signal that Mrs Bracken sent to her daughter.

Suddenly the child broke into bright smiles. 'Of *course* I remember, Mummy. I *never* forget.' She withdrew a few steps from Ted so that he could see her better and broke into some elementary, but well-executed tap while she sang:

> 'I'm a snowflake, just a snowflake,
> and I've fallen from the sky for you.
> It was cold up there,
> but I didn't have a care,
> I just fell out of the blue.'

There was a pause in the singing while the tap became more elaborate and frenzied, and then she went on:

> 'I've been falling quite a while,
> I should think at *least* a mile,
> not just down,
> but in love with *you*.
> So if you have a heart,
> just keep a tiny part,
> for a lonely little snowflake true.'

When the song, and the appallingly explicit gestures that accompanied it came to an end, Fern finished with a curtsy and her right hand approximately where Mr Strong might suppose her heart to be. Unfortunately, she had danced herself off the parquet on to the corner of a valuable rug that Ted was particularly fond of, and as she stumbled over it she lost her balance and slid unerringly on her bottom towards an eighteenth-century marquetry table set with ivory chessmen that he had been planning to send to Sotheby's in the next appropriate sale.

Mrs Bracken rose to her feet. 'Oh, my goodness me! Whatever have you done, child?' She yanked Fern to her feet, dusting chessmen off her as though they were huge breadcrumbs while she apologized on Fern's behalf, 'She's ever so sorry, Mr Strong: she knows it's a dreadful thing to have done, she'll be crying her eyes out when she gets home, if not before.' She had begun to set the table to rights, as Ted desperately rescued a bunch of pawns. When he put them back in their place on the table – fortunately undamaged at first glance – Fern put a timid, bony little hand on his sleeve.

'Mr Strong – I'm so very s-sorry for what I've done. I didn't mean it, honestly I didn't. I'm s-so s-sorry.' He saw to his amazement that huge tears were coursing down her face, which looked the picture of frightened despair. Her voice, too, had dropped nearly an octave, and the slight stammer made him feel for her.

As he put the last few pieces back on to the table, he said, as heartily as he could, 'Never mind, no harm done.' He looked to make sure that the set was complete, and then turned to Fern. To his dismay her tears had not stopped, and they were only punctuated by little gasps of indrawn breath.

'Look, Fern, it's all right, I've forgiven you.'

'H-have you, *r-really*?'

'Of course.'

'Then – have I g-got the part?'

He laughed uncomfortably, conscious again of Mrs Bracken's homing in on this question like some sort of hawk. 'Well, naturally, I can't tell you anything about that, yet. It's quite a part, you see, for such a young child: I shall have to complete auditions and discuss the matter with my producer.' He turned to Mrs Bracken and saw her do the opposite of being relaxed. 'I'll let your agency know, Mrs Bracken, of course.' He looked at where his watch usually was, and found that he had forgotten to put it on. He looked at his wrist again to make sure: to make sure, also that Mrs Bracken had received the hint. About thirty seconds after he had begun to be afraid that she hadn't or wouldn't, she did.

'Well, we really ought to be going: I don't like Fern to be out late in this weather unless she has to be because of working. She's delicate: sturdy,' she amended, 'but delicate.' While Ted was digesting this remarkable variety of constitution, Fern had begun to climb into a mock-fur poncho with a hood, and Mrs Bracken was twitching her hands into gloves. Ted put some lights on the stairs, and saw them gladly to the front door, resolving never, *never* to audition a child and its Mum without someone else to support him. 'Only then, I'd laugh,' he said to himself as he bounded upstairs to get himself a Scotch. As he sat down with it, he wondered fleetingly whether the children enjoyed their extraordinary but boring lives. Probably; children loved attention . . .

In the street, Mrs Bracken grasped, rather than took Fern's hand and they plodded sharply on to their first bus towards home. She was completely silent, which was worse than her immediately talking, Fern knew, because it meant that when she *did* talk, she would talk more. 'If only she'd leave me alone,' Fern thought, and then tried not to think of anything else.

It wasn't until they were in front on the top of the bus, that Mrs Bracken began.

'. . . getting clumsier every day. I don't know I really don't know what you're coming to. You might have broken all those knick-knacks and then where would we have been?'

'I did cry when you told me to. I cried a long time.'

'You did that, and it may, I don't say it will, but it *may* have made that tiny difference that makes *all* the difference.'

'I can't do that silly dance and song any more. I'm too old for it.'

'None of that from you. You're eight, and don't you forget it. I wish you'd stop trying to grow up all the time. It doesn't suit your type at all. You still look podgy on top in that smock.'

Fern scratched one of her painfully bandaged breasts – they always felt bruised and itchy these days – and wished that she went to a children's acting school like the rest of them, and didn't just have classes with her mother there all the time. 'When I have to do my "O" levels they'll have to know,' she said, as childishly sulky as she could manage. The only way to bring her mother round was by acting like a baby. Her mother snorted.

'Only the people concerned will have to know. The agency won't say anything, because they won't really know, and if they look like finding out, we'll move.'

'I want my tea,' Fern wailed quietly. It was true, she did want it, she was always hungry, because her mother wouldn't ever let her have bread, or potatoes or even sweets or ice cream. It would be cold stewed apple and two slices of ham, and one triangle of processed cheese with a glass of grapefruit juice. She was so hungry now, that if she had her piece of gum with her she would have chewed it. But as usual, she had left the gum on the third banister from the right just under the rail – a place that combined being easy of access with being difficult to find for anyone who didn't know it was there. But her mother would notice if she chewed gum. Her mother noticed everything, like people said God did, but her mother was never friendly and helpful in the way that some people said that God sometimes was.

'. . . money doesn't grow on trees . . .' her mother was saying. If God wanted her to believe in him, all he would have to do would be to put some money on the bare plane trees – nothing to him, if one was to believe a word he said – and her mother would be proved wrong, and then nothing would ever stop Fern from believing in God *all the time* and taking no notice of her mother.

'Fern's hungry!' she wailed again, more childishly than before.

'Fern will get her nice tea as soon as she's home.' From her mother's mollified tone Fern knew that she was thinking of her own nice tea as well.

Her mother's nice tea consisted of three crumpets, toasted on both sides and soaked in butter and celery salt, a huge piece of Viennese chocolate cake bought from the local *pâtisserie* and a cream doughnut. This was washed down by three cups of sweet, hot tea with the top of the milk in it. Fern always sat opposite her at meals and the table was sharply divided down the middle in the sort of food that was displayed upon it. On Fern's side would be the protein and the Vitamin C; on her mother's, the carbohydrates, fats, and sugar. Fern knew so exactly how bad everything that her mother ate was for her, that she, Fern, was sometimes dully surprised that her mother never seemed to get ill or weak – seemed rather to wax larger and heavier month by month; a box on the ears was no light punishment these days, and as she grew older the boxes had become more frequent as well as more painful.

Now, her food finished, having asked for and been refused more, she sat, not allowed to get down, watching her mother munch her way through the doughnut, licking sugar and cream off her fingers and wondering which bit of her mother was going to bulge more as a result. The trouble was that her mother didn't seem to bulge with fat, but simply with hard, heavy, muscle; she became steadily more formidable rather than formless.

After tea, Fern was allowed to 'play' for a short time until she had to do her exercises. Usually, this meant sitting on the floor with dolls or a picture book. Her mother varied, but for days at a time she would seem to pretend that Fern couldn't read, and only give her books for babies. Fern had got to the point where she really didn't know whether her mother was pretending or had actually forgotten: arguing invariably produced a rage, and taking no notice was usually easier. Sometimes Fern wondered, quite indifferently, whether her mother was mad. For instance, she encouraged

Fern to read in French, which seemed dotty, as they had hardly any French books in the house.

Tonight, when she had got down, and was listlessly looking at a huge book about an elephant (which she knew by heart) there was an odd noise coming from the back door – a kind of scratching scuffle. As her mother was out of the room, she went to see.

It was a small black, brown and white dog – not any particular kind of dog as far as she knew. It was sopping wet, cold, and extremely friendly. Fern let it in, and then quickly got a tea-cloth to dry its wiry wet fur. It licked her repeatedly – its tongue felt boiling beside its icy nose. It had kind brown eyes and was very thin. Her mother came into the kitchen just as Fern was finishing the drying process, or rather just as the cloth had become so wet that there was no point in going on with it. Before her mother could say anything, Fern rushed up to her mother, flung her arms round her and said, 'Please, Mummy, darling Mummy, let's keep the poor doggy for one evening. It's so dreadfully hungry and I promise to take care of it – Mummy?'

'The child's face was transfixed – transformed,' Mrs Bracken quoted hurriedly to herself: 'Well, just for one evening, then,' she said aloud, smiling so that Fern could see the top gums of her artificial dentures as Fern called them, having been told not to say teeth – it was common.

'Can I give it some supper?'

'If you must.'

'What shall I give it?'

'Well – there's some milk, and some stale bread in the bin: otherwise it would have to be your breakfast ham ...' The telephone rang, and Mrs Bracken went purposefully off to answer it. Nothing was ever allowed to come between Mrs Bracken and the telephone. She would sit in her telephone chair – nice and soft – and light a cig with one hand while she was picking up the receiver. She had a voice she kept specially for the telephone. There it was now: 'Hailloagh?' it had begun.

Fern got some milk out of the fridge, and then decided to take the chill off it. She poured quite a lot into a saucepan: the dog was looking at her and making little mewing noises of ravenous gratitude. It knew she was making it a meal. She got the old loaf out; it was *so* stale that she had to run it under the warm tap before she could break it up, and by the time she had done that the milk was warm enough. She got a bowl, poured the milk carefully over the bread and set the bowl by the fridge. The dog gulped it down so fast that there was nothing left in a few seconds, but feverish licking went on and on round the dry, shining bowl. Then the dog looked at her, wagged its tail, walked over to where she sat on her heels the other side of the table, and sat down in front of her, at the same time thrusting a paw into her delighted hands. In the next room Mrs Bracken was saying things like, 'Why *should* you? I should pay no regard to *that*,' and 'Well – they know who to blame then, don't they?' Fern put her arms round the dog's neck – he had no collar and he was a he – and hugged him. He responded with heartfelt enthusiasm. When she asked him whether he was hungry, he instantly looked agonizingly hungry. 'You shall have my ham,' she promised him, and he kissed her with several kisses getting faster and faster. She gave him both slices of ham in the end, but she broke it up into pieces to make it last him longer. He simply loved ham. He kissed her a good deal when it was finished, and then uttering a sigh so deep it almost sounded theatrical to her, lay down, put his head casually on his hind legs, and slept.

By the time Mrs Bracken had finished her telephone conversation (her friend had a daughter called Pearl and had been having trouble with a manager over panto) and had pretended aloud to Fern that she would find Fern doing her exercises in the Studio, Fern had also fallen asleep – leaning against the dog in the kitchen. 'Well I never!' said Mrs Bracken, whose better-tempered remarks always sounded as though they were being made to several people – none of whom were Fern. 'And what's become of our exercises, may I ask?'

Fern woke up, saw her mother, and then felt the dog, who had woken up the moment Mrs Bracken appeared.

'Can he come too?' she pleaded, and pleaded was the word.

'Just for this evening,' Mrs Bracken allowed, while further noisome clichés and catchwords ('Inseparable! Her dumb friend') churned about in her mind for possible future use.

The dog sat quite quietly watching Fern do her bar work, and her general limbering up which ended with doing the splits: if she spoke to him, his tail wagged gently and at once; otherwise, he endured the metronomic records that Mrs Bracken put on a small box-gramophone, and her shrill commands or incitements to do things harder, more slowly, or again.

The Studio was below the flat where they lived, and although it belonged to them, Mrs Bracken had to let it out for dancing and drama classes. Many a child had been taught to put its hands on its knees before it smiled in that room; to repeat questions on such a shrilly upward inflexion that it masked the total lack of incredulity; to produce 'expressions' at the drop of a cue and to get slick with continental clichés. It suited Mrs Bracken very well: it meant that Fern had nearly all her classes in safe custody, as it were. Mrs Bracken had once tried running classes herself, but had stopped quite soon for lack of pupils. It was in any case far easier simply to let the place than to try to teach kids anything.

When she had taken Fern through her evening exercises, Mrs Bracken sent her up to bed with her supper, which consisted this evening, as nearly always, of an orange, an apple and a banana. Tonight, however, there was also included the dog. Mrs Bracken knew so little about animals of any kind that the basic implications of keeping the dog escaped her. Fern could take it to bed with her – why not? Anything to keep her quiet was often Mrs Bracken's motto, particularly as it got near her own supper-time. So Fern unobtrusively let him out among the two dustbins and privet that filled most of the garden, and then took him up with her.

Her room was small, dreary, and uncluttered by personal possessions. Fern got no pocket money, and, seeming to have no relations (her father was dead, not, Mrs Bracken had added with mysterious venom when telling her this, that it would have made any *difference*) and she not only had no aunts or cousins, she had also no friends. Mrs Bracken saw no point whatever in friends: she had a few people she chatted to on the telephone and met in the agents' office – other mothers, like herself – but otherwise knowing people any better would have meant having them in the home, feeding them, and embarrassing things like that. You didn't want to get too familiar, she said to Fern, who by now had little or no idea what she meant. So there was nothing in Fern's room but a bed, a huge wardrobe with very few clothes in it, and one or two children's books. The evening ritual began with Fern having a bath, during which time her mother usually left her alone, although, if she had been 'bandaged', as Mrs Bracken put it, her mother would undo them. Tonight, however, Fern had the idea of bathing the dog to make him nice and clean for bed, as he had a slight smell of railway stations about him, and she was willing to put up with bandages until after supper if she could get the bath over before her mother found out.

She made the bath much cooler than she liked it, as she felt the dog would probably dislike hot water. She had imagined them both in the bath together, one at each end, but when it came to the point, she realized that it would be more practical if she put him in by himself. She lifted him up and dumped him as gently as she could. He gave a strangled squeak, his tail went between his legs; he looked at her and shivered. She kissed him and then began the battle of washing him. This could only be done by fits and starts and with one hand, because if she did not hold his neck fur, he made spasmodic but frantic plunges for freedom. He looked more waifish and ratlike than ever when he was thoroughly wet, but she felt that beneath or inside his appearance, he was really quite pleased to have so much attention. Rinsing him was awful; hundreds of tooth mugsful of clean water were poured over his quivering body before she felt that she had got the soap out. Then there was the frightful job of drying him. She was soaked through in no time, while he remained extraordinarily damp. In the end, she finished him off on a clean towel she took from the cupboard. By the time he was done and snugly wrapped up in her dressing-gown at the end of her bed, delicious smells of Mrs Bracken's TV fry-up were rising (the kitchen, like the studio, was on the ground floor). Tonight, Fern could smell onions, sausages, tomatoes, eggs, and, she thought, chips. Oh Golly! Tonight she was not the only one. The dog's nose was oscillating with the keenest appreciation, and he cast her one or two urgent glances to see what she proposed to do about it. When Fern asked him if he was still hungry, there was no doubt about the answer: extremely hungry. Eventually, Fern felt that for his sake she must be brave. She put her dressing-gown round her shoulders, told him to stay on her bed, and tip-toed down.

Her mother stood with her back to the gas cooker, her feet turned slightly outwards, so that her unexpectedly narrow ankles looked even more extraordinary with the huge calves flexed above them.

'Please, Mummy – '

Mrs Bracken did not turn round.

'Could you undo me please?'

Her mother turned the gas down with a heavy sigh and did turn round. 'Heavens! Haven't you had your bath yet? Whatever on earth have you been doing?'

'I've washed – ever so carefully. But, please – ' her mother was now twitching away at the bandages, 'could the dog have something for his supper?'

'You've just fed that dog.'

'Before my exercises.'

75

'Give him some of your fruit then.'

'Dogs don't eat fruit. They don't like it.'

'Miss Know-all! He'd eat it if he was hungry enough.'

'I love him. I don't want him to feel as hungry as that.'

'I told you – give him some of your ham.'

'I've already given it to him. And anyway, Mummy, dogs have to have their own food. You know, like dark red meat, and dog biscuits and everything.'

'If you think I'm keeping that dirty creature in the house –'

Panic-stricken, Fern gave ground. 'All right, Mummy, actually I've washed him so he's lovely and clean.'

'What are you standing about for then?'

('Because I'm so hungry I could easily eat dog biscuits myself, and after your tea you're having an enormous real supper so why can't I, and why can't the poor dog have the same? Why shouldn't we all have enough to eat and a nice time?') What she actually said was: 'Nothing,' and trailed forlornly upstairs. She was dreading having to face him with nothing.

He was very nice about it, really *good*, she said to herself. His look of expectation about supper turned into a look of expectation about seeing her, and he kissed her with evident delight at their reunion. It was much easier to go to sleep with someone who felt the same. When she put out the light, he waited a moment, and then crept up to her end of the bed and settled himself in her arms as though this was how they'd always been together.

The day, though, was not at all like the night. This became cruelly apparent at breakfast the next day. On Fern's plate was the tomato she would have had with the ham she had given to him. Beside the plate was her glass of milk and her half grapefruit. It was another cold day, and the sight of this meal minus her two slices of ham made her feel shivery. She hesitated, then asked her mother if she could have some more ham (there *was* more, in the fridge, as she knew); her mother said no. She asked if she could have a boiled egg then, or some cereal, and her mother said certainly not, whoever did she think her mother was?

Fern sat at the table, with the dog beside her. Tears filled her eyes and spurted out on to her empty plate. The telephone rang, and her mother surged out of her chair to answer it. As soon as she had gone, Fern cut a slice of Hovis, and, with her mother's knife, spread it thickly and quickly with some marmalade. He ate it with discreet speed, and she had time to lick her fingers and collect the crumbs from the bread-board. Mrs Bracken came back just at the end of this, as though she had been waiting in the wings to be told.

'Mr Strong *is* considering you for the part,' she said. Her smile had more teeth in it than she usually bothered to display in the home. Fern knew she was pleased, and wondered how to get something for him out of it before anything went wrong.

'There's many a slip betwixt cup and lips,' her mother said, as though she knew exactly what Fern was thinking. 'I gather a child he had in mind went down with measles. He will want to see you again on Friday.'

Today was Tuesday. Surely, before then, she could get him accepted? He needed regular proper food, walks, a collar and lead, tons of love – if *only* she had pocket money! She spent the rest of the day coaxing, wheedling, trying to get her mother to love the dog, and to do something about him. Her mother accepted these efforts with bland satisfaction, but she continued to behave as though the dog did not exist. Fern tried to keep him with her, as she was afraid that her mother might be nasty to him if she was not there to protect him, but when he growled at people coming to classes, she was forced to take him up to her room and shut him in there. By evening there was a real crisis. Fern, having gone without her breakfast, and half her lunch, was desperate for her tea or supper, and so was the dog. But when she explained this to her mother, Mrs Bracken simply said that *she* had not wanted the dirty creature in the house: if Fern wanted him, she would have to be responsible.

'But I haven't got any *money*!'

'Oh, it's money now, is it? Whatever next! First you have a dog and then you want money.'

'Only to feed him with. He *must* have food or he'll starve to death.'

'I don't care what he does. And kindly leave the bread alone. It's new: far too good for him, and you know you're not allowed to touch it.'

Frantic, Fern cut up the pieces of ham on her plate, unwrapped the small triangle of cheese and broke it into pieces. The dog ate it in about five seconds, looked at her appealingly and wagged his tail. He was clearly asking for more.

'You understand, that's your lot for the night.'

Fern looked at her mother, and to her utter confusion, saw that Mrs Bracken was almost smiling – as though she was enjoying herself! How could she be? – in such an awful situation! But it needn't be like that at all! It was her mother who wasn't allowing everyone to have enough, while she guzzled away without having to share a thing. And she could do anything she liked, because of having money and being grown-up. Her eyes filled with tears, and furious that she couldn't help it, she said as a retort: 'If you're not careful, I'll be so hungry, I won't be able to see Mr Strong on Friday, and you won't like that!'

Her mother's reply was to take the dog by the scruff of his neck, and kick – literally kick – him through the back door into the night.

'That's that, then,' she said. 'Finish your fruit juice and up to bed with you.'

Fern burst out crying. It was icy cold, and rain or sleet was falling to make things worse. He had nowhere to go; he was lost, and now, without enough dinner, he had been pushed out and he would either get run over or freeze to death.

Her mother boxed her ears: Fern threw her grapefruit juice on the floor. For a moment they both stood staring at each other, panting, each wondering what outrage the other would commit next. Then Mrs Bracken seized Fern by her hair and started to pull her out of the room: Fern kicked the bulging calves of her mother's muscular legs, but owing to the rounded toes of her shoes and her long hair, her mother easily won. At the top of the stairs, Fern tried once more:

'If you don't let him in, I *won't* eat anything and that will make me no good at the audition. You'll see.'

'Silly nonsense.' Her mother practically threw Fern on to the bed (she was frighteningly strong sometimes), slammed the door, and then locked it. Now, she wouldn't be able to creep down when her mother was asleep to let him in! He would be out all night, and would probably go away, if he didn't die of cold. Cruelty to animals; she would like to have her mother arrested for it if only they did that sort of thing. Once she was sure that her mother had gone, she cried more quietly out of sheer misery for him. Her bedroom was the wrong side of the house: it looked out on to a main road, so she dared not call him. She considered trying to escape down a drain-pipe, but there didn't seem to be one near enough. Eventually she fell asleep for a few hours, and when she woke up she remembered that there was a Society for the Prevention of Cruelty to Animals. She should have remembered this before, because she ought to have known that her mother would be Cruel to him, and not waited for her to be it.

Her mother let her out of the room in silence: there was nothing in her face to tell Fern how things were. When she went down to the kitchen, her breakfast was laid out, but before sitting down, she went to the kitchen door and opened it.

He was there! He had waited. He was wet, bedraggled, and shivering, but his ecstasy at the sight of her had no resentment at all. She flung her arms round his neck and he whimpered with joy. Surely her mother would see how sweet he was? She had one last try. 'Mummy – look, Mummy, he waited all night. Please can he come in?'

'It's nothing to do with me,' her mother replied levelly, as she placed her own steaming plate of breakfast on the table.

'Can I dry him a bit?'

'As long as you don't use any of my towels.'

(As though the house was filled with other people's!)

In the end, she used rather a lot of paper towel, and he did not seem to be very much drier, although grateful for the attention.

She looked at her breakfast – wanting it quite badly – and then began to cut up the ham.

'If you're going to mess about with your food, I'll put it away.'

So that was why she hadn't seemed angry. She'd been waiting to say that! What she meant was that if Fern tried to give any of her food to the dog, it would be taken away from her. In fact, he was not to be fed at all. He was to starve to death. That was worse than being cruel – it nearly amounted to murder. If only her mother had actually murdered a person, then she could ring up the police and have her taken away – as easy as that. But animals didn't count – except to the Society . . .

She ate her breakfast – there was no point in nobody having it, and she had to think what to do and if she got too hungry she wouldn't be able to think about anything. After breakfast, and after classes began in the Studio, she knew her mother would have gone out to shop and have coffee and more cakes with someone or other. So, she asked to be excused, went quickly to the telephone and dialled the operator (she was so bad at spelling that looking things up was hopeless). The Royal Society, etc., it turned out to be called. She memorized the number (she was good at remembering things) and got on to them.

It took her some time to explain what she wanted. They seemed to find it difficult to understand why, if she was *there* – where the dog was – *she* couldn't do anything about it. 'I'm a minor,' she said more than once; 'you see I can't stop any of it because I'm a minor.' In the end they agreed to come.

The same thing happened at lunch. Her mother said that if she did not immediately get on with her meal, it would be taken away. She took her supper out of the fridge while her mother was on the telephone and hid it until she could take it up to him (she was keeping him out of the way – in her room as much as possible).

Mrs Bracken came back from the telephone. 'Mr Strong will be seeing us this evening with a friend of his,' she said. 'I'll wash your hair.'

This was a familiar but horrible business. First a trickle of icy water on her head – icy to scalding – then soap in her eyes, nothing to get it out with, then feeling that she was drowning as her mother poured huge enamel jugsful of water of indiscriminate temperature over her, then being violently rubbed with a specially harsh towel followed by the near-weeping pain of being combed out with a steel comb and her mother's temper on edge, to the final misery of being screwed so tightly into curlers that it felt as though her hair was being very slowly pulled out by the roots … it was one of the worst spots of the week. The whole process took a little over an hour but it seemed to change the whole day. When it was all over, her mother made her sit at the kitchen table and do homework of one kind or another.

The kitchen was the warmest room in the house, and Fern liked being there. She would also have liked to have the dog with her on this of all afternoons, but she dared not do it, in case her mother ordered him out of the house. All the afternoon, she longed for and dreaded Them coming!

They turned out to be one youngish man. There had been a Keep Fit class in the studio that afternoon, so Mrs Bracken didn't answer the door-bell when it rang. Nor did Fern. She had put a head-square on, but her curlers still bulged and peeped from under it. The class was over and people were arriving and departing continuously, but when Fern heard a man's voice asking for Miss Bracken she knew who it was, and went to meet him. She asked him to wait in the kitchen. 'I'll fetch the dog,' she said and ran very quietly and quickly up to her bedroom: with any luck, her mother would be still snoring her 'short afternoon rest' away.

The dog cringed when he saw the Inspector, as he called

himself. That did not seem to matter, however; the trouble was that he kept asking questions that Fern couldn't answer properly. Who did the dog belong to? If she, Fern, liked him, why couldn't he stay with her? What did Fern think was wrong with him anyway? He seemed all right – a bit on the thin side, but if he was a stray ... At this moment, Mrs Bracken entered the kitchen. She had an expression that Fern knew and hated. There was no more problem about answering questions.

'My mother wouldn't give him any food, you see. So he hardly gets anything, except some of mine. It isn't enough for either of us.'

'And what, may I ask, are you doing here?'

'He's an Inspector about cruelty to animals.'

'The R.S.P.C.A., madam.'

Mrs Bracken's face went blank.

'I don't remember asking you to come.'

'No, madam, it was your daughter.'

Mrs Bracken turned her impassive gaze towards Fern: then she shut the door. 'Oh yes?' she said, and sat down in her mealtime chair.

'The situation is perfectly simple, madam,' said the young Inspector, but having said this, he could think of nothing more.

'The dog's a stray,' said Mrs Bracken. 'Nothing to do with me.'

'I understand that your daughter is quite – '

'It's nothing to do with her, either. I've told you – the dog just walked in here, dirty thing, and has hung about ever since. I haven't given him the slightest encouragement.'

'It's my fault. I gave him a lot of encouragement. I liked him.'

'No collar or nothing?' suggested the Inspector, hopelessly.

'Nothing at all!' Mrs Bracken's triumph suggested that dogs commonly wore or had hung about them innumerable clues to identity.

'You haven't tried the local police station?'

'Why ever should I do that?'

'The point is that *she* won't give him food at *all*. Don't you see? He gets no food unless I give him some of mine, and that only means we're both hungry. You'll have to take him with you!'

There was a short silence. The whole business had something funny about it, the Inspector thought, but he hadn't got all day. He took the collar out of his pocket and moved over to the dog and the little girl; the dog cringed again. The girl bent down and stroked his head, and he kept still while the collar was fastened. He looked to the Inspector very like one of the innumerable dogs – mongrel – whom owners get tired of the moment it has stopped being a puppy: they were everywhere these days, including motorways. What some people would do to their animals beat him, it really did.

When he straightened up with the dog on the lead, the little girl asked him: 'What will you do with him, now you've got him?'

'Well – we shall try and find his owner – wait a bit to see whether anyone comes for him – '

'And if they don't come?'

The Inspector looked at her. He had thought her ridiculous when he first saw her, but she seemed to have changed. 'We'll try and find him a nice new home,' he said. He was afraid she wouldn't leave it here, and she didn't.

'And if you can't?'

'Oh – we'll find someone – don't worry,' he said. As usual, when he told people lies, he looked her straight in the eye. Just as he felt that she had thought it over and was beginning to believe him, the mother, stupid cow, said:

'Oh well, if you can't find him a home, you'll have to put him away, won't you? He's only a mongrel, after all.'

After a second, the little girl said to him: 'You don't do that, do you? Kill them, I mean, to stop people being cruel to them? You *never* do that!'

'Stupid *cow*,' he thought again: surely she knew better than that? He tried to give her a warning, quenching, generally silencing look, but it was he who quailed when *she* met *his* eye.

'No – we don't do that,' he said, with all the authority he could bring to the statement. 'I must be off,' he added, as it occurred to him that the stupid cow could also turn out to be a muscle-bound bitch. 'Do you want to say good-bye to him?'

'No. Yes, I do.' The little girl bent down by the dog, who seemed very fond of her, kissed him, and said, 'I hope you have a lovely good home.'

The Inspector left as soon after that as he possibly could. He could see that the child was nearly crying and he dreaded another catty outburst from the mother. It was only when he had put the dog in his van that he realized that really he'd simply wanted not to be present when she started . . .

'. . . using the telephone behind my back and creating these scenes! Have you lost your tongue or something?'

'Yes! I don't want to talk to you.'

'If we go on like this, we may not get any supper.'

Fern said wearily, 'I wouldn't get any anyway. I gave it to him. I'm going to bed.' She walked past her mother and out of the room. '*That* settled her,' she thought mechanically. It always outfaced her mother to find that a threat had become empty, as it were, behind her back.

In her bedroom it was plain to see where he had scuffed himself a nest of eiderdown to sleep in. She threw herself on the bed: for the first time in her life she was neither afraid nor simply distressed, but urgently miserable. If there had been a bolt inside her door she would have bolted it. She felt as though she had never had a chance until the dog came, and when he left, all the chances she might have had were suddenly impressed upon her. Lots of children lived marvellous lives with a father and brothers and sisters, as well as animals: she had known this for a long time through classes and jobs in studios where there were other children, but she had never compared herself to them because it had seemed silly even to try. But now – because she had lost the dog, she realized that he was all she had to lose . . .

A long time later *She* came in, and said that Fern could have some tongue and scrambled egg if she liked. Fern said she didn't want it – leave her alone. To her surprise Mrs Bracken did leave – without the usual voice-raising argument ending with a threat. 'I just thought in view of your interview,' she said, but when Fern repeated, more sulkily, that she didn't want anything: that was that.

When she was sure that her mother was having her supper, Fern cried for the dog. She kept repeating to herself that the Inspector had said that they didn't kill dogs to stop people being cruel, but the more she thought about it, the less sure she felt that this was true. What could they *do* with dogs that people didn't want? If it was true, then her mother was a murderer. This thought gave her surprising satisfaction – funny, you wouldn't think that you could bear to think that your mother was a murderer, but she *liked* thinking it. She had always known there was something horrible about her, and this was what it was. Before she went to sleep, she undid all her curlers, and combed out all her hair with a wet comb. There wouldn't be any ringlets for the audition.

In the morning, her mother cried whatever-had-she-done-to-her-hair, but the tones were of powerless dismay, and not the usual frightening voice that led up to her losing her temper. So at breakfast, Fern refused eggs and bacon in her new, cold, sulking voice, and to her amazement, her mother asked her quite quietly what *would* she like. A cup of black, sugared coffee, she said. She had to have something or she'd faint, and black coffee struck her as the most sophisticated choice. She got it, didn't like it, but managed to sip it down gazing into a new distance – not her plate, nor her mother, nor the wall – but somewhere incalculable, a place that certainly did not include her mother. She refused to talk at all, except at the end of breakfast, when she announced that unless her mother bought her a pair of jeans and a sweater and proper shoes, she would not go to the interview at all. And *that* worked as well, as easily as anything! Her mother took her out and actually got them – even a black sweater (which she had always wanted) and red moccasins. Fern brushed out her long straight hair without any parting and clipped it at the back of her head with a tortoise-shell slide. She looked at herself: everything was much better, if only she didn't go on finding herself wondering whether the dog was all right, and what was being done to him. Each time she wondered that, she found it easier to be as horrible to her mother as she could think of. Because of all the shopping they had to go a large part of the way to Mr Strong's (South Kensington) by cab . . .

When the door-bell rang, Ted Strong thought it was Jake – round to support him over the Bracken girl interview. Then he saw through the frosted glass that there were two figures on the doorstep, and his heart sank. It was bad enough meeting Mrs Bracken at all, in *any* circumstances that he could possibly think of; meeting her with that pathetic backward precocious child of hers was worse, and meeting her for a *second* interview – when clearly she must think her child's role was in the bag – was worst of all. But the truth was that he had left the whole thing too late – treated it far too casually, and now he was paying for it. He'd been so pleased with himself over the casting of the old man and the middle-aged couple that when the producer had started some grotty argument about the script, he'd turned all his attention on to winning that without seeming to, and he simply hadn't thought about the child's part – more than that there *was* one – until about ten days ago. Since then, after hours of nightmare, he had found only one child he thought really suitable – and Fern Bracken (God! what a name!). The suitable one had of *course* got measles, of *course*, so now, given how little time there was left before filming actually started, he was more or less saddled with Miss Fern Bracken. And her sodding awful mother, who reminded him, he remembered, of some over-upholstered gym-mistress-cum-sadist-cum-lesbian? Or bird of prey. Or something. By now he had opened the door and saw to his relief that Jake was paying off a taxi beyond Mrs Bracken and Fern.

'Good good. All arrived together, I see,' he said.

'Good morning, Mr Strong. Say "good morning, Mr Strong".'

The child looked at him – very coolly, for her age – and said: 'Hullo.' Behind her, Jake was extravagantly miming his sorrow at being what amounted to late. Mrs Bracken turned from the door to look at her daughter, and would have nearly caught him had he not stopped instantly as though frozen or shot.

After that they all trooped into the dark hall that Ted had not decided yet how to decorate, and Jake took off his suède-and-beaver coat, while Mrs Bracken declined taking off anything. This made Ted wonder whether if she had stripped off her gigantic herringbone beetroot tweed overcoat she would seem less awful, because that must make less of her, or whether if you could more clearly see what less of her there was it would be nastier. Fern simply stood quietly until they moved upstairs.

Upstairs, Ted had a good look at her. She seemed taller, older, and far more – well, more of a *person* than a category. Either she had changed drastically, which seemed impossible in less than a week, or his powers of observation were flagging. He remembered the snowflake routine and swallowed – no, he had rightly been attending also to Mum, and *she* hadn't changed at all. There she was, establishing herself on his sofa and crossing her ankles in that particularly unwinning manner.

He picked up the script: Jake balanced himself on an Italian chest and pretended to stare at a picture by Fuseli, whom Ted knew he loathed, and Mrs Bracken leaned – ever so slightly – forwards.

'If you want me to read anything, I would rather do it alone with you.'

'Right!' This was his cue – mad not to take instant advantage. 'Jake! I wonder whether you'd take Mrs Bracken upstairs and give her some coffee.'

It was surprising how easy everything suddenly became. Jake, although he gave Ted one look that combined astonishment with imminent revenge, got Mrs Bracken to her feet and herded her (she really was someone who suited this collective verb) up the stairs, out of sight, and finally earshot.

The moment that he heard the door upstairs close, he turned to the girl and found that she was staring at him so urgently that he could notice the shape of her eyes: they were not childishly round as he remembered.

'You're not really eight, are you?'

'Of course not. I'm twelve – nearly.'

'Why does your mother say you're eight then?'

'Because she's wicked. She's probably the most wicked person you've ever seen in your life!'

'Oh, come now!'

'What do you mean? She *is*. She's cruel, too. There's a Society isn't there? I don't mean the animal one. For not being cruel to people. Have you heard of it?'

'Yes. Well, there's the Society for the Prevention of Cruelty to Children.'

'If you reported her, where would they put me?'

'My dear girl, *I* can't report your mother for anything. I know nothing about her. I think we'd better get on with –'

But, without his noticing, she had moved up to him until she was barely a foot from where he sat on the arm of the sofa. She clenched her hands and then shook them in a recognizably theatrical gesture:

'Report her! You've got to! Once you know that someone's as wicked as that, you've got to!'

'As wicked as what? Look here, Fern, what does she do to you?' Perhaps there might be something in it, after all. The poor child couldn't help her gestures; they'd probably been dinned into her since she was a baby.

She took a deep breath, and he could feel her thinking.

'She – she washes my hair so that it hurts. Boiling water, and the soap gets in my eyes. She won't ever let me have cakes or anything like that, but *she* eats them all the time. I don't go to a proper school because she won't let me. She never gives me any pocket money. She's always making me do dancing exercises and go to class and practise horrible French and that. And when she smiles, it only means she's being more cruel than ever! It's not fair!'

Ted relaxed: the final cry, ubiquitous to all the children he had ever encountered – even his sister's children about turns on the pony – on top of what seemed to him typically child-ish resentments, showed quite clearly that Fern was only griping about what was probably too much attention from her mother, and possibly a stricter discipline than ordinary children encountered. Of course the wretched little creature hadn't *chosen* to act: almost certainly her mother had de-cided upon the career for her, and all those mothers became obsessed with pushing their children in what they con-sidered to be the appropriate directions.

Fern, who had watched him to see his reaction, realized that she had not had the desired effect upon him.'She beats me! With a big wooden spoon! Every night she does it!'

'Now Fern, I think you're exaggerating. In any case, if you want to do this audition without your mother, you'd better get on with it.' He picked up the script again, and pretended to be studying it to give her time to cool down a little. She gave a sharp little sigh, but when he glanced at her she was looking at him quite steadily – seemed calm as though nothing had happened. He explained to her what he wanted her to do, and she listened with surprisingly professional attention. 'What age am I supposed to be?'

'Let's say about ten. I don't think you could play anything younger than that.'

'Not unless I was a silly snowflake.'

He looked at her, and just caught a wary, flitting little grin. He'd never thought of any of them as having the slightest sense of humour.

'It's not snowing today,' he agreed smoothly. 'Now – let's see what you can do. Remember, when you wake up – at first – you don't even know where you are.'

'On the floor?'

'Fine.' He chucked a pillow from the sofa.

She lay on the floor with the pillow tucked under her head, and did what he'd told her – woke up in a strange house wondering where on earth she was. 'Now, start calling for your Aunt.'

It was not at all bad. She didn't hurry the waking up, and she moved well. Her voice wasn't so hot – the years of training to be cute and shrill had taken their toll. He told her to do it again, and to use her ordinary voice: 'how you'd call out if it really was you.' At once she complied, and there was nothing wrong with her own voice. He made her do it once more, telling her this time a little more about the scene, to find out how she took direction. The third time was all right. She had a kind of throw-away intensity – if you could put it like that – that would suit the part very well, and he felt that he could quite easily get very much more out of her.

'Right,' he said, after the third time. 'Well done. That'll do nicely for now.'

She picked the cushion up from the floor and advanced to the sofa with it, one hand brushing back her hair.

'Do you want me then?'

He had already made up his mind, but he pretended to do so now – 'Yes. Yes, I do.'

'Right. But I'll only do it on one condition.'

'Oh now Fern, I am *not*, repeat *not* going to report your mother.'

'It's not that.'

'What is it then?'

'Get my mother down, and I'll tell you.'

There was no trace of childish hysteria: she was absolutely calm – and determined. He found himself calling Jake on the intercom and a few minutes later the room was full of Mrs Bracken again.

For a fleeting instant, Ted wondered whether the whole thing was worth it: instinct told him a scene was on the way, but every other child he had seen had been indescribably worse than Fern . . . no, he hadn't any choice.

'I think Fern will do very well for the part,' he said, smiling generally in Mrs Bracken's direction (he could not meet her fishy grey eyes); 'but she seems to want to say something about it first.'

Everybody looked at Fern, who stared straight at her mother.

'Yes. I had this dog, you see, but Mummy wouldn't give me any food for him, and so my food wasn't enough for both of us so in the end I had to get the R.S.P.C.A. to come and fetch him. But I'm pretty sure from how the man was that they won't find him a new home which means they'll have to assassinate him.' She turned to Ted. 'Another cruelty, you see!'

'Fern, whatever are you talking about!'

'*You* know perfectly well. I'm telling Mr Strong. If you don't get the dog back and promise on your honour to buy him proper dog's food, I won't do the part! I won't *ever* do *any* part. And however much you don't give me any meals or anything it won't make any difference because I'll get you reported to the R.S. People Society. That's what I'll do. And what I *won't* do,' she added for full measure.

Mrs Bracken got to her feet: she was smiling, but uneasily.

'You know what quaint ideas they get in their heads,' she said to Ted and Jake. 'Over-excitement, I've no doubt, and she's got ever such an imagination. Come along, dear, we must be going home.'

'Not till you've rung up the Society. You've got to do it now. In front of Mr Strong. Or I won't do his part.'

Mrs Bracken smiled harder. Jake said casually:

'Why not give them a call? I'll find the number for you.'

He was rewarded by a smile from Fern so brilliant that Ted saw for the first time what she might be like when she was grown up.

'I don't know what's come *over* you,' Mrs Bracken was saying beneath her breath, but weakly.

'Would you like me to make the call?'

'No. She must do it. Thank you. She must ask for us to be able to fetch the dog now.'

And Mrs Bracken had to do just that. What with her anger, the audience, and the fact that she clearly felt that she had no choice, her telephone voice went to pieces. She sounded quite nervous and conciliatory. But while she was dialling the number, Ted observed that Fern was even more nervous, and went over to her.

'You mustn't bite your nails,' he said gently. 'You've won, so what are you worrying about?'

'They may have – they might already have – you know.' Her face looked pinched with anxiety.

'Assassinated him? I don't think they would have done that till they were sure they couldn't find him a home.'

'I do hope not.' Her intensity was such that he began fervently to hope not also.

They hadn't. The dog was available, and when Mrs Bracken had turned to the room with ready-made benevolence to convey this, Ted said: 'Hang on a minute.' He walked over to the window, seized the telephone and said, 'If you'd put the dog in a taxi, I'll pay for it.' There was some demur at this, and he had to go into his top gear of high-powered charm. In the end, he sent Jake in a taxi to fetch the dog, and Jake, surprisingly, went with the minimum of implied martyrdom. When he got back to Fern, who had gone to the far end of the long room, he saw that she was silently crying.

'All's well,' he said as heartily as he could. Then, uncomfortably remembering something, he said, 'Like something to eat while you wait?'

She swallowed and then looked at him so eagerly that he knew he was right – or rather that he *had* been wrong. 'Sausages, eggs, bacon, fried bread?' he said, trying to make the most of the meagre choice available.

'Oh yes, *please!*'

'Perhaps your mother would like to pop round to the shops to get the dog's food while I knock it up for you. We can have a nice quiet talk about the part while you're eating.'

He looked commandingly at Mrs Bracken, who now smiled, or at least showed her teeth if anyone looked at her. It worked. Mrs Bracken seemed quite broken-in. She murmured something about having some shopping to do anyway, and went.

Upstairs, in the kitchen, his breakfast things were lying on the table and she said:

'Could I eat just a spoonful of that marmalade?'

'Help yourself.' Then he looked at her. 'Are you all right?'

'A bit dizzy. Can I use its own spoon?'

'Here – have a piece of bread – or toast, if you like.'

'Aren't I going to have it fried?'

'We can run to more than one piece.' Children of that age are always hungry, he thought – rather uncomfortably.

There was a shortish silence while he fried things and Fern ate.

'All right?'

'Lovely. I'm eating it especially slowly because my dog eats so fast. He hardly gets time to enjoy his food.' Then, with no pause at all, but as though she was breaking entirely new ground, she said, 'I wanted to ask you something.'

'Is this another of your conditions?'

'Not – exactly. But I wondered whether you could pay *me* some of the money I'll be earning. You see, if you pay it all to *her*, I don't get any, and with the dog I'll be needing it, I really will. He wants a collar and a lead and one of those medal things with his address on it and a towel to dry him when he's wet and I want to keep a sort of emergency amount – '

'Look, Fern, I don't pay anybody – someone else does all that. I couldn't possibly arrange to split your salary up.'

'Oh.'

'Cheer up – here's your nosh.' He put in front of her a

93

plate that looked like the advertisement for some famous sauce.

'Can I start?'

'Feel free.'

There was another silence while she ate and he watched her.

'When did you last eat?'

She looked up. 'Lunch – yesterday. She wouldn't let me give it to the dog, so I ate it, or she'd just have taken it away. She locked him out in the rain all night. I *told* you she was wicked. If I could just fill in a form and leave her, I would.'

Ted lit a cigarette. Mrs Bracken was undoubtedly a disagreeable old bitch, but he didn't want to get involved. 'You can't do that,' he said.

'I know I can't.'

'Look. Here's a fiver. To start your dog off with.'

'Oh – Mr Strong! Oh – *thank* you!'

Poor little thing, she seemed quite overwhelmed. Hell – he *was* getting involved.

'I'll never forget you. What you've done for the dog,' she said.

'Anyway – you've won with your mother – hands down.'

'I haven't finished yet. I've just started really.' She put half a tomato on to a piece of fried bread and into her mouth and chewed contentedly. 'I used to wish sometimes that she was dead, but now I don't. Not now I know what to do.'

'How do you mean?'

Her knife and fork were poised in the air, and she spoke dreamily. 'I don't want to kill her any more – I want her to stay alive and get slowly more and more miserable. I'm going to end up being to her just like she was to me. I know how to do that now.'

Ted, startled, stared at her and she smiled, but her eyes were grey and cold as a fish.

THE PROPOSITION

ROBIN BOSTON-CRABBE had scarcely brought the Mercedes to a halt before the commissionaire had a white-gloved hand on the door-handle of the car.

'Good morning, sir.'

'Morning. All right if I leave her here?'

The commissionaire clearly hesitated.

'I have an appointment to see Mr Medusa.'

The commissionaire's face cleared. 'Certainly, sir. You know your way, sir?'

'No, but I imagine it's at the top.'

'Right, sir. But it's not on the board. I'll ring through for you, sir.'

While he was doing this, Robin read the gold-painted names of the other occupants of Dorado House, as the luxury block was called. He also noticed that there were two lifts, that nobody got into or came out of either of them, that there were live goldfish in the pool round which a number of opulent ferns were grouped, and that there was no sign of a staircase or even of a door that led to one.

'Sorry to keep you waiting, sir.'

Robin had already moved towards the lifts, but as he was about to press a button to summon one, the mirrored panel between them swung gently open.

'Mr Medusa has his own lift.'

'So I see. Thank you.'

The walls were covered in cork flecked with gold and there were only two buttons. One said 'up' and the other 'down'. Robin pressed the 'up'.

In the lift he had time to feel nervous. This was the opportunity that so many waited all their lives for in vain: if he made the wrong impression now, he would never get another chance. He had dressed with care and he wore clothes well – had several times been asked, in fact, to model for some high-class advertisements that involved standing about in blazer or tweeds outside a country house leaning on a sports car or being leaned on by a red setter but, naturally, he had refused. He had always been careful of his image and, judging by this morning, it seemed to have paid off.

The butler was waiting for him; of course.

'Good morning, sir. Mr Medusa is expecting you.' He opened a red leather door and led the way down a passage lined two deep with Paul Klees. A further red leather door led into a very large sitting-room, studded with pots of flowering shrubs. A huge fireplace contained a log fire – burning now with some aromatic fragrance.

'If you will be seated, sir, I will inform Mr Medusa of your arrival.'

But Robin was too fascinated by the room to sit down in it. Apart from the pictures – Chagall, Soutine, de Staël, and others he did not recognize – there was a beautiful T'ang horse, and a silk rug in apricot and yellow. There was also an enormous pedimented mirror (Chippendale?) with amazingly carved cupids and fruit. He advanced upon this to have a final check-up of his appearance. His hair had really been very well cut; he smoothed it back and gave himself a tentative, encouraging smile.

At that moment, a low, voluptuous growling began – like prickly velvet, and Robin turned sharply on his heel to find his host a few yards away and accompanied by the largest Alsatian he had ever seen.

'Mr Robin Boston-Crabbe! Be *quiet*, Felicity! I cannot say she is perfectly harmless – she is not. But she will do as I tell her.' He advanced to the fireplace and pulled a green silk tassel. Then he stood, a small, frail figure, wearing a superb tussore silk suit, with his back to the fire, surveying his guest in so penetrating a manner that Robin's general nerves accentuated to a specific shyness. The Alsatian subsided watchfully on the hearthrug and the butler reappeared.

'Ah, Ipswich. Champagne, please. If that suits you?'

'It sounds great.'

'Do sit down. You look in wonderful shape. Skiing evidently agrees with you.'

Robin smiled. He always knew exactly what shape he was in, but he liked to have it noticed.

'As a matter of fact, a film producer in Gstaad actually asked me whether I would be interested in appearing in a film he was doing.'

'Really? And what kind of film had he in mind?'

'Oh – one of those dear old super-spy epics.'

'How amusing! How extremely funny!' Mr Medusa's heavily hooded, almost turquoise eyes screwed up while he laughed. He was, Robin decided, not only a very striking man, but possessed of exceptional charm. It was impossible to determine his age. He realized that Mr Medusa was again regarding him closely, and said, 'I was admiring your wonderful plants.'

'Were you really? Well they *are* a joy. It is so teasing of camellias not to smell, but I've managed to get my chap to bring on the stephanotis to be with them. The best of both worlds, which is really the only point of having a little money. Give us a glass each and put the bucket next to Mr Boston-Crabbe, Ipswich.'

'I suppose it is.'

'Oh – come – you don't do too badly. That watch you are wearing would not lead one to imagine you are confined to supposition. Or perhaps it was – given to you?'

Robin could not help glancing at his Patek Philippe. 'As a matter of fact I bought it.'

Mr Medusa brought the palms of his hands together with a small papery thud. 'There you are! It is my opinion that you are quite rich enough for your age ... One could not wish you to become – spoiled – in any way. But I admire your watch. I really do.' He raised his glass – the champagne was very nearly the colour of his hair. 'And what shall we drink to?'

Robin felt himself almost blushing. He must not seem un-
enthusiastic; he must not presume – he did not know what to
say.

'Perhaps we should drink to the memory of poor Le
Mesurier.'

Robin bowed his head and they both drank. Ipswich had
left the room.

'You were with that gentleman for some years, I believe?'

'Nearly five.'

'Ah yes. And I have been told from – several sources – that
he always found you most satisfactory.'

Robin nodded, and kept his expression grave but reliable.

'Well! We won't rush things. What were you enjoying
most about this room when I came into it? Apart from your
own charming image, that is?'

Now he felt he *was* blushing. He mumbled something
about the plants.

'You mustn't mind me. I'm a terrible tease. And you *do*
look perfectly charming. Yes, I always have flowers growing
as a matter of principle. Do you realize that all cut flowers
are simply dying before one's eyes? And not only dying,
probably dying a most slow and disagreeable death. A dis-
gusting thought. I have never understood how people can
stomach it. Death, when it has to come, should be in-
stantaneous, don't you think? But of course you do. Could I
trouble you for a little more champagne?'

When Robin bent to pour from the bottle he noticed that
Mr Medusa's lightly tanned face was completely smooth –
not a wrinkle or a fold of flesh to be seen.

'A good, steady hand,' Mr Medusa remarked approvingly.
'But then, one would expect that. I have one question
to ask you – of a somewhat delicate nature. Oh – do help
yourself.'

Robin did so, and then sat on the edge of his chair opposite his host.

'When you were with poor Le Mesurier, I take it you were
– exclusively – with him? I have no wish to pry into any

arrangements there may have been between you beyond this one point.'

Here it was: the one question that he had dreaded – that in all his private rehearsals of this interview he had been unable to decide how he should answer. Tell the truth, and he would be out on his ear: lie, and in all probability he would be detected and out on the other ear. To his surprise, Mr Medusa was not looking at him, was merely gazing intently at his champagne. He took the plunge.

'I did once go off – but the whole thing was only a week-end – it was before I realized Mr Le Mesurier's feelings in the matter, and after that I never did so again.'

There was a short silence, and Robin, already regretting his choice, added rather desperately: 'It was only once, and that's the truth.'

Then Mr Medusa did look at him. 'I know. I was afraid you might lie and I never look at people when I feel they may do that.' He drained his glass and held it out for more. 'I think we shall get along very nicely. You will have plenty of time to get used to my ways. I shall not want you to kill anybody for at least a month.'

Robin let out his breath.

'Thank you very much, Mr Medusa.'

THE DEVOTED

JAMES stirred – stretched out of the pitch-warm ditch until his foot struck one of the hard, cold animals who slept in rows each side of him. 'Polar,' he thought, and opened his eyes. The new dark was cold and fresh and stinging, and he moved farther, beyond Polar, down his bed. His mind whirred, working slowly up to waking, and suddenly struck. Christmas morning! For a moment he lay motionless – stiff with the gorgeous certainty of the high-pitched, mysterious crackle at the end of his bed. *He* knew how it got there: nothing to do with Father Christmas; one father was enough, by Golly. People crept in before they went to bed and put it there. His sister, Van, thought one's mother ought to be Father Christmas, but she thought of nothing but mothers – or rather their mother. People said she was morbid. He did not know what the word meant: a sort of mixture of too much and too bad – a really grown-up word like stair-carpet. He hoped very much he'd be morbid himself one day.

It *was* dark! He sat up: it was awfully cold. He would be fish-cold in a minute. 'Frozen to the spot,' he hissed aloud, hoping to wake Van, but there was no sound from her. He had asked to sleep with Van. 'She cries at night and she likes me there,' he had explained. Really it was the only way he could borrow her watch, which was large and round with a second-hand that worked; Van cried every night while their mother was away, and he timed her. He let her cry for nine minutes and gave her thirty seconds to stop. Then he had to give her back the watch, and they both went to sleep. At home he had to share a bedroom with Marie-Laure, who smelled of parsley and prayed for ages and tried to make him talk French.

He was beginning to freeze. He felt about with his feet until he found the creaking bulk of his stocking. He imagined exactly how it lay for a moment, and then plunged for it – flinging himself head downwards. He hit his head on the iron rail and said 'Ouch' more loudly than it hurt, but there was still no sound from Van. Somewhere in the stocking would be a torch, but not, he betted, at the top. 'Bet your life no,' he said aloud. Wake her up, she's only a girl, even if she is older, he thought. He could feel the tangerine and, he thought, the chocolate money. He'd eat those and pinch the paper together to make flat old money. He was shivering with hunger, and rage at the dark, and Van still sleeping. Christmas ruined already: he was sick of looking forward to things. 'You may get a train for Christmas, if you're good.' Think of saying that to someone who was anyway going to spend their life driving engines. 'Unfair,' he muttered, and hurt himself grinding his teeth. *Un*fair – *un*fair – *un*fair – he jolted up a steep incline of resentment, louder and faster, till he got to the top and thought he might shriek. Better not: wake the silly French thing next door. He leapt out of bed and ran to Van, stubbing his bare foot in the dark. Painful tears streamed easily down. 'Van! I had to wake you up! I'm hurt! I've hurt half my leg!'

He felt her wake, instantly attentive. She switched on the light. He hopped before her, holding the bad foot, frowning to keep his tears moving. His hair stood in tufts like spare grass.

'Poor James. Did you have a dream? It's cold! You must be freezing!'

'I am. I'm like new ice-cream. You'd freeze to death if you touched me.' He pushed his fingers under her hair like a small bunch of keys on the back of her neck. 'Stop your nose bleeding.' She squeaked, and he danced with joy.

'It's Christmas! It's morning! Get yours, and let's open them.' He rushed to his bed and held up the end of his stocking.

Van looked at her watch. 'James, you know it isn't even six

o'clock. It's really still night-time. You know they said not till seven.'

He stood up on his bed bouncing gently with rage.

'I'll yell. I'll tell them what you cry about. I'll put your beastly watch down the lavatory and pull the plug. *Whoosh!* It'll be gone just like that! Done by me!' He nearly fell over pulling the plug. He leaned forward impressively. 'I'll be *sick* at breakfast. Widely sick *next to you!* I'll swallow my pudding sixpence and then I'll have to live in hospital and you'll *never* see Mamma because she'll live in hospital with me and Dad. You'll be alone for the whole of your life – a thousand years at least. Well?'

That worked. Her eyes filled with tears; he saw her imagining the thousand years. He sneezed, and said:

'But if we open them now I'll be so nice. I'll be on your side all day. I'll kick Desmond if he teases you, and I'll help you bury your best present.' He sneezed again.

Van leapt out of bed, 'Put on your dressing-gown, then. You'll catch your death of cold.' She said it crossly.

Robed, they stood glaring at each other, with the bargain not quite clinched.

'You promise, James? You absolutely promise?'

He hesitated for the most convincing word.

'I – *morbidly* promise.'

Her face cleared. 'O.K.'

They leapt on to their beds and seized their stockings.

'Happy Christmas,' he said, carelessly tearing at his top present: he was radiantly happy.

Vanessa left him sitting in a sea of coloured *crêpe* paper and tangerine skins, eating her chocolate money (he had finished his own) and pulling to pieces his best thing – a clockwork frog. He was wearing a black beard, a patch, and a bus-conductor's ticket-machine slung over his dressing-gown. His animals were arranged in a double row at the end of the bed and he was quietly boasting to them about the frog. He was perfectly safe to leave to Marie-Laure.

She dipped her flannel into the icy jug and rubbed her face. She had to do her hair in one plait because she had lost the other elastic band. The photograph of her mother in her Presentation dress, with white feathers, very black thin lipstick, and fat, long, white gloves, watched her while she dressed. The picture was not at all like her mother, but she accepted its appearance as an alien, almost mystical extravagance: her mother could look like anything and be always the most beautiful of all people. Her watch said ten minutes to nine.

She, James and Marie-Laure – the visitors – slept on the top floor. Downstairs was the floor on which her grandmother, her uncle and aunt and her cousins slept. Here were two staircases, one at each end of the corridor: the children called them major and minor. You slid down the banisters of major and chased Ruby, giggling madly, up and down minor. Groucho, the black Labrador, lay at the bottom of minor, and thudded his tail mechanically at her approach. With a deep sigh he heaved himself up and jostled heavily against her down the passage to the garden door – their difference in weight was like wrapping up her outdoor shoes in tissue-paper, she thought.

The door had their heights marked against it, with dates: she and James always spent their holidays here, but usually their Mamma had spent some of the time with them. They had never spent Christmas Day without her – but this time Dad was really ill and she might not be able to join them at all, she had said.

'If we *put off* Christmas Day, could you?'

'Darlings – we can't do that. But I'll ring you up specially – at tea-time – how's that?'

'That will have to do, then,' Van had said stiffly, wanting to cry so badly that she hated Dad – *hated* him. Christmas without Mamma seemed to her an unbelievable disaster: pretty well the worst thing that could happen in the world. The very worst thing, something dreadful happening to her Mamma, had for so long now been her chief preoccupation and terror that she had become quite business-like about it. One gave things up – adventures, presents, chocolates, anything at all nice whenever Mamma was away, in return for getting her back safely. So far it had always worked. Of course, one had to balance what to give up against the length of Mamma's absence – the bargain had to be fair; but she had had years of practice because Dad had been ill – off and on – ever since Van could remember.

Outside was bright grey – breathlessly cold – but without snow. 'I'm *glad* there's no snow,' she thought, crunching the frosty grass with her feet. It was the most anti-Christmas thing she could think. Groucho was following her, pretending to be very faithful. 'First we're going to the potting-shed, and then to the dirty old Place,' she told him, and he wriggled self-consciously, as though she had paid him a compliment.

The potting-shed smelled like slightly burnt rich cake, and was beautifully, neatly untidy. 'You can't be really tidy about earth,' she thought, 'except at a distance.' The thought pleased her. 'What old thoughts I have to myself. No: I mustn't be pleased. Really I'm awfully sad – I simply save up my crying and do it all at once, but my sadness is spread over the whole day.'

The dirty old Place was behind the kitchen garden, through some laurel bushes where was embedded a vast disused water-tank in which they played 'Prisons', a gloomy, domineering game invented by her oldest cousin – and finally to an ash-heap. Beyond this was a small stretch of rough grass. Here she was going to dig the grave . . .

It was a grave designed for her most extravagant expectations in the way of a doll (with real hair – which was the whole point). Surveying it, she felt that nobody could be expected to be any kinder than that. (The grave was about three feet long.) She knelt down to smooth the frozen, lumpy earth, so that the doll – whoever she was – should be more comfortable. 'I hope she won't have a name,' she thought.

'With a name she would have to die. If she hasn't got one, I can pretend she's dead already.' She sat back on her heels. 'I'll put her here as soon as I can escape after they've given her to me. I'll try not even to look properly at her first. I won't sing in church; I won't have bread sauce or mince-pies; I'll kiss Desmond under the mistletoe; I'll give my cake icing to James; I'll even pull bare crackers; if the doll is small I'll put my second-best thing in as well. She *must* ring up at tea-time, and if she doesn't say she's coming tomorrow, she must at least come before the end of the holidays.' She paused, and shut her eyes tightly to stop the tears coming out. 'And nothing awful is to happen to her – nothing – specially not catching whatever Dad has got. Nothing awful is to happen,' she repeated.

It was done: she walked slowly back. If the doll was small but had long golden hair, surely she needn't put her second-best thing in the grave as well?

They had all gone to church. Marie-Laure, because naturally she was a Catholic, must wait until evening for her church. Someone was going to drive her there. They were very kind, and she wished very much not to be so stupidly afraid and silent, but she seemed very little better at speaking English now than five months ago.

She had thought that she would be home for New Year – through all these lonely, homesick weeks her heart had been set upon it – but now, with this fresh illness of Madame's husband, she knew she should stay. 'Surely she can procure for herself another nurse for the children!' wrote her mother from France – but Marie-Laure knew that this was not so, although she dared not explain to her mother why. She attempted to explain the goodness of Madame, but of the terrible drinking of Madame's husband she dared not write. Until she had arrived in this family, Marie-Laure had thought that men like Madame's husband did not exist except in the books of a nature which she was not supposed to read. Indeed, at first, she had not perceived anything to be wrong. Madame had been kind and charming, and he had been perfectly correct to her. But in scarcely a week she had heard him making Madame a scene, at night – when the children were mercifully asleep, but she, Marie-Laure, had heard the shouting and the big sound of something smashed. Much later, Madame had woken her and told her to take the children out for the whole day – to return only in the evening. When they had come back, Madame's husband was not in the house, and Madame had explained everything about Monsieur, and implored her to stay because the children had suffered from too many changes of persons in charge.

Since the war, he had become like this, Madame had said. For weeks he would drink an infinite number of bottles of Coca-Cola, and then suddenly he would be out for hours – drinking somewhere out of the house – and then the scenes would start all over again, and either Madame would take him away to be cured, or Marie-Laure and the children would be packed off to stay somewhere else in London, or here, with Monsieur's brother. Each time Madame had said he might this time be cured, and each time when he returned, pale and subdued, and charming to Madame, Marie-Laure had prayed that Madame's faith might be answered. But, alas – no; each time no, and her pity for Madame's terrible life increased, and fought with her private war of homesickness, which seemed, like her English, and Monsieur, never to get better.

In London, except for the brief, ravishing confidences of Madame, Marie-Laure was alone with the children (the little boy teased her, and spoke too fast, and the girl was jealous of her when Madame was there, and listless when she was not). She lived for the letters from France: for news of her sister's baby, for the mosaic of domestic detail which made up her home; wept at a distance for the death of her canary, marvelled at the magnificence of Madame Grandet's funeral, and longed for a proper soup, and her own church, and for the inside of a house to be warm.

She was ironing the best dress of Vanessa: pale *café au lait* – very pretty. These people were rich to have so large a house so crammed with heavy furniture. They had more money than Madame, but heavens! they were dull! It was unbelievable that the red-faced Monsieur could be the brother of Madame's husband – so pale, so attractive, in spite of his sinful life. Had she been Madame, Marie-Laure reflected with sudden fear, she would have selected the drunken brother, not the good red dull one. She sighed. Sometimes she was a little afraid that everything good was dull. She hung up the freshly ironed frock: soon the big black dog would bark and the letters would come. How terrible for Madame to be spending this day in hospital. She wished very much that she might be as beautiful as Madame. Then, she thought, I would have a house the envy of all. My legs would be thinner, my husband might even admire them, and bring me flowers. Already she was eighteen – so soon all this might occur in her life. The big black dog barked ...

At the very last minute Ann had decided not to go to church with the rest of the family. There was so much to do, she said to her husband: she seemed always to be saying something of the kind to him. Keeping the ponderous extravagant wheels of the household moving, even slowly, took all her time and energy: precluded her riding, watching him shoot (he adored her to watch him shoot), playing tennis or golf with him, or even going to London for an occasional day with him to watch cricket (a game which she never understood, and which invariably gave her a splitting headache); in fact, prevented her from anything which had been originally designed as their mutual interests. Today there was a great deal for her to arrange ...

She walked slowly upstairs, remembering the look of patient masculine incomprehension on Donald's face as he tucked his mother carefully into the front of the car. I'll take off my hat and get out of this skirt – it's far too tight on me since Janet, anyway – and see if Ruby really understood that she must clear the dining-room for luncheon *before* she starts on the bedrooms, and get Mrs Bond to speak to Spragg about the water being cold again this morning, and try to get Marie-Laure to clear up the nursery bedrooms a bit for Ruby ... it was so like Lillian to employ a series of girls who were no use in the house and didn't speak a word of English. The irritation, which she always felt and was ashamed of when she thought of her sister-in-law, interrupted her plans for the precious time when everyone was out of the house.

Ruby had not understood. As Ann approached her bedroom she heard the shrill, tuneless crooning – in American overlaid by Gloucestershire – which Ruby, who was never without a wireless except in the bedrooms, employed while making the beds. 'What would I dew – without yew?' etc., but the moment Ann opened the door Ruby gasped a brilliant pink, apologized inaudibly, giggled and made a tumultuous exit with mops and brushes, and a hail of Kirbigrips. Ann sighed, called Ruby back, explained again to her about the dining-room and asked her whether she had seen Marie-Laure. Ruby couldn't say for certain, but she fancied she was ironing, and Mrs Bond had said if Ruby showed her face in the kitchen before half past she'd have kittens. This was Mrs Bond's ultimate threat, which, though biologically improbable, masked, as everyone in the household knew, a state of mind and temper which it would be dangerous and silly to ignore. 'Clear everything on to trays on the sideboard, then, Ruby.' Ruby said, 'What a pity there was no snow,' and went.

Ann shut the door after her, sat down at her dressing-table and was horrified by how tired and harassed she looked. Her hat was awful. She laughed weakly at it, took it off, and ran her hands through her hair. She ought to do something about her appearance generally, if it came to that. After all, it was Christmas Day, and here she was, married, with three children and an unusually nice house. Nobody could call Donald an exacting or difficult husband.

Her mother-in-law was extraordinarily good about the difficult business of living with them. Of course they had plenty of room, which helped. Ann was devoted to the house, and she really liked living in the country – it was only when she was tired, or when she compared her life to Lillian's, that she felt discouraged and a little lost. But the sight of Lillian, haggardly attractive, intelligently debonair, had always roused her to some kind of dim resentment, and now, even Lillian's children or her mother-in-law's long-distance anxiety about their father produced the same effect. Russell had always monopolized the attention (and anxiety) of everyone near him. He certainly monopolized mine, Ann thought – for as long as he wanted to do...

She had just returned from three months at a school in Paris, where she had learned some French, some dress-making, some cooking and a little enthusiastic party patter about the French Impressionist painters. After that, her mother proceeded to buy her a lot of clothes which she had been in Paris long enough to despise, but not long enough to alter, and sent her to parties. At one of them, she had met Russell. He had listened to her discoursing on the relative merits of Van Gogh and Cézanne, and had then, with no compunction whatever, tripped her up by introducing a whole lot of names of what she had assumed to be more painters; told her after she had made a fool of herself that they were impressionist composers, and said that she was pretty enough to be honest about her ignorance. 'I burst into tears,' Ann thought, struggling out of the tight skirt, 'and then he started to be nice to me. I don't believe I've even thought about Van Gogh since.' Certainly, for months after that she had thought of nothing but Russell. They had met again by chance at another party at which Russell had played the piano most amusingly for hours, and Ann, taking no further chances, and filled with the delicious self-confidence that sometimes permeates the young, decided to collect him. She thought him so wonderful that some of her ardour communicated itself to him, and eventually he found her discerning, imaginative, a good listener and, she still desperately believed, pretty. His future at that time was to be a doctor; probably, they thought, a brilliant surgeon: even after he had failed his first exams, twice, she believed that. Meanwhile he did everything else with a facility and charm which she found dazzling. She began to imagine herself married to him. Of course he would have to pass these examinations first. But he didn't. The second time he failed was the first time that she saw him drunk. An indirect result of their first and last row was that he met Lillian. He simply picked her up at a party, and that was that.

Ann had been asked to the wedding, and in a fever of despairing masochism, went. There she met Donald, drank a little too much champagne and actually cried on his shoulder. She went out with Donald several times after that because he comfortingly combined being Russell's brother with not looking in the least like Russell. And now here she was. She had Desmond, Roddy and Janet – and Donald. Lillian had Vanessa and James – and Russell. Ann had the large lovely inconvenient family house, and Lillian had a neat little house in Pembroke Square. Donald managed the farms, and Russell lurched with varying degrees of reformed pessimism from job to job. Her children, though not particualrly distinguished, bless them, were nice, healthy, normal children, whereas Vanessa was a distinctly morbid little girl, and James was utterly spoiled. On the face of it, Ann had everything to be thankful for, and poor Lillian had very little. Heaven only knew how she managed their permanently rocky finances, the endless humiliating situations with other people, the monotonous exhausting scenes with Russell, without becoming a wreck. But she *did* manage all of it admirably. She had simply acquired a steadiness, an intelligent tact, an enduring perceptiveness about Russell, which enabled her often to avert and always to smooth over the repetitive worst moments. This poise seemed to have fined her initial glamour to an elegance, to a charm the penetration of which far exceeded any effect which Russell, even at his best, could provoke. In fact, what disturbed Ann was that living on her perpetual edge of anxieties and misfortunes Lillian contrived to become more attractive, interesting and amusing, while she, Ann, ensconced upon the broad plains of secure domesticity, seemed to herself to have become almost anonymously dull. 'My features look as though they've run into each other – I haven't got a bad figure, I simply haven't *got* a figure, and when we do meet people, I can't think of anything to say to them. Perhaps Lillian *likes* the drama of it all – she'd probably be miserable if Russell wasn't there to make trouble.'

She was battling with an extra leaf in the dining-room table; pinching her cold fingers (the central heating was nil – oh dear, the boiler again): but she immediately knew that such reflections were spitefully unfair, and, deeply ashamed of herself, she went to stop Groucho barking at the poor postman, who was terrified of dogs.

An hour later, she walked slowly round her dining-room table with a pride and delight which even the stern fringe of last-minute touches could not conceal. Decorating a table was much more exciting than icing a cake. Now it gleamed with all the Christmas fruits: the fat embroidery of pineapples like stump work; clementines; pale green silky apples; oranges and bananas like china; freckled bulky pears; nuts like tight brown satin, like brown boulders, like Oriental eyes, like commas, like maps of estuaries at low tide; dates packed in glistening treacle-brown sprays with their decorous paper-lace pelmets; wooden boxes of magic fruits crystallized for a hundred years; peppermint-cream in crisp frilly green, and Turkish delight in a haze of white sugar. The ranks of glistening glasses, and the stiff bright white of the napkins, the circle of finger-bowls each starred with a small white chrysanthemum, the small red candle and horseshoe roll beside each place had all been arranged by her until she had made a perfect setting.

'There is still the Tree to finish,' she thought, 'and the Present Chairs, but otherwise ...' and quite suddenly, she began to enjoy the day, forgetting, as she forgot every year, that she never enjoyed Christmas until she had arranged the luncheon table. Groucho barked again – she heard the car – their voices – even the timing was traditional. Each year she thought there would never be time, and each year there was enough time for the table, and just not enough to powder her nose ...

The children had all been packed off with the French girl for a walk, poor little devils, but considering what they'd sunk in the way of food and drink, perhaps it was just as well. Donald had herded them out of the dining-room himself. 'And no sliding down major till after tea, or I'll horsewhip the lot of you,' he had roared unconvincingly, glaring up at them from the foot of the stairs.

There had been a gale of laughter, and then James, the highest up the staircase, had cocked his head on one side and announced: 'Hollow laughter: like in books,' and screaming, scrabbling, teasing one another, they had rushed away.

'It's amazing how food simply galvanizes them: like stoking up a lot of little boilers,' he remarked on re-entering the dining-room. His mother smiled gently; his wife said, 'So unlike our boiler.'

She looked tired, he noticed: she *would* do herself up on these occasions. He put a hand heavily on her shoulder, waited a moment and patted it. 'Have some brandy, old dear, and stop worrying about the boiler.

She shook her head. 'There's tea to do, and the Tree and the Present Chairs.'

'I can do all that,' he said helpfully. He was not at all sure that he could. 'Let's relax for a bit. I've eaten so much I can't move. Mamma: brandy?'

His mother put her little, fat white hand over her brandy glass.

'Oh – come on, Madam. I can't drink all by myself.'

His mother's hand contracted over the top of her glass, and he thought, 'Oh, Lord; another brick, I suppose. Damn Russell.'

'We will all have a little,' said his mother. 'We will drink to Absent Friends.'

'Right,' he said – a little too heartily, and poured the drink.

Ann said, 'I want very little, please,' and lit a cigarette. Donald thought for the hundredth time, That's one of the things I've never told her. Nobody is allowed to smoke in the dining-room without asking Madam first. Except Russell, of course.

His mother was saying, 'When I was a young girl, the servants were never allowed to wash up on Sunday afternoons ...'

The toast, somehow, was not drunk.

After his mother had been persuaded to rest until Present time, he returned to find his wife still sitting amid the Christmas litter, smoking, drinking her brandy, and eating a peppermint-cream. This nauseating combination touched him: but because it exposed an area of his emotions which he somehow could not bring himself to express, he laughed and said: 'Really, Ann, you're worse than the children!' and saw her flush defensively, before she replied, 'Sorry. I wasn't thinking.'

He sat down, and poured himself some more brandy. 'Don't be silly. It's Christmas, after all.'

'You mean I can be as silly as I like?' Then she saw his glass and exclaimed, 'Oh, Donald, *don't* have more brandy!'

He was suddenly, unaccountably, angry.

'How many times do I have to tell you that my drinking a reasonable amount on these occasions – *not* every day and all days – but occasionally having a couple of drinks doesn't automatically mean that I am taking to drink? I'm not like Russell – never have been, for better or worse.'

There was a short pause, and then he added, 'Sorry. But if there is one thing calculated to drive me into becoming like Russell, it is being watched and nagged every time I do have a drink.' And she answered steadily, 'I wasn't thinking of him. I was only thinking about your inside, and the doctors saying that brandy was the worst thing. I know you aren't like Russell.'

He stared heavily at her; seeing, not her face, but only a reflection of his inability to be gay or sensitive, brilliant or commanding; to avoid this ritual recurring pattern of misunderstanding between them. He stretched out his hand to her, but the table was too broad; he could not reach her, and she made no move. Helplessly, he said the last, hopeless thing: 'I expect you wish that I were.'

The rooms Donald's mother occupied were unlike the rest of the house. Apart from the rearrangement of furniture upon which she had insisted when her beloved Alec had died (his dressing-room was now her bedroom, their bedroom was now her sitting-room) she had slowly accumulated a concentration of the smaller, more personal objects which in her day had been strewn all over the house: the photographs, the framed pieces of family embroidery, the bits of china, and the little presents which darling Alec had always brought back to her from his travels. The walls were comfortably crowded, the furniture made movement in the room a circuitous business: there were four clocks and eleven little shaded lamps, and (but it was an aroma so essentially her own that she was not aware of it) the rooms smelled always of bread and butter, and lavender, and Russian leather, and beads. In this elaborately encrusted shell she spent much of her time – and here time seemed to move for her, although perhaps only as a gentle, rhythmical backwash: the wake of her own ship slowly coming home. Outside, even anywhere else in the house that had been hers for forty-seven years, she felt like a stopped clock – not broken, but stopped for ever in 1936, when darling Alec had died.

The immediate agony and terror had vanished, and now each day calmly occurred, leaving her with a kind of faint astonishment and awe that she could complete it without him. That was her past. Her present, her future – all distant, incalculable anxiety – was her eldest son: so physically like Alec that her heart turned over when she saw him; in character so incomparable that she ached with responsibility and shame. The last discovery that she and Alec had made about one another had been when he was dying, and they found that each had known of Russell's instability, and each had striven for years to conceal it from the other. The last revelation had illuminated their whole marriage for them: he had died entirely loving her, knowing that he was entirely loved.

Then she had been left with Russell, at that time half-heartedly engaged upon a job with some advertising firm. On his father's death she had appealed to him to come home and manage the estate. 'Living in the country would drive me nuts, Madam. Let Donald do it, and divide the swag.' Then he had kissed both her hands with a gesture which belied his words, and added, 'My dear Madam! There is no woman living for whom I would even consider leaving London – excepting yourself – but I *have* considered it, and it would be no good. I should be bad and bored. I shall frequently descend upon you, and Donald will be quite happy being a gentleman farmer. He's cut out for the life.' Which was perfectly true. Donald was cut out for it, and did seem, on the whole, happy.

Then, three years later, the war. Russell had immediately joined the navy, but Donald, poor Donald, had proved to have something so wrong with his inside that no service would take him. She reflected with a certain amount of guilt that the only time in her life when she had really cared desperately about Donald had been a night during Dunkirk when he had actually broken down and wept at what he felt was his own futility. He had thereafter farmed himself to a standstill of fatigue, while Russell had become a small-boat commander. As one by one his fellow officers were killed, and as she watched him on his leaves, intent, excited, living always at a tension which it seemed impossible to her he could sustain, her perpetual fear that he too would be killed became complicated by the curiously persistent thought that perhaps it might be better if he were: at least he was filled with the energy of happiness and success. But he emerged from the war with a D.S.C. and two bars, and she never discovered how many mentions in dispatches; knocked about a bit, played with the idea of being a doctor, broke a few inexperienced hearts, met Lillian, and married her privately and at once. Paying off his debts, she had taken the opportunity of warning him that marriage was totally unlike war, and that she would not be able to continue rescuing him financially. He explained at great ingenious length how neither the war nor Lillian bored him, how he only drank when he was bored, and swore that he would henceforth stand on his own feet, and so on.

It was years later before she discovered that Donald had paid off the same debts . . .

She had begun by disliking Lillian, but, although they had never succeeded in any great degree of sympathy, she had been forced to admire Lillian's loyalty to Russell, who, it must be admitted, had run the gamut of impossible behaviour. Their children, in spite of it all, were far more interesting than Donald's rather dull little crowd – James, a third edition of Alec; Vanessa, a taut, tense little creature, all eyes and bones and secret reserves. She had taken more trouble with Vanessa's Christmas present that she had with all her other presents put together – going to London to choose the doll herself, and then making its clothes elaborately, like the clothes she had worn when she had been a child.

Her clocks struck three one after another; she admired their split-second independence. It was time for the Presents. Of course she had not rested; she had merely concentrated her present anxiety into this privacy, so that it was concealed from the others. 'It's a bad bout this time, I'm afraid,' Lillian had said on the telephone. 'Yes, of course, I said I'd ring Van anyway on Christmas Day, so I'll tell you more then.' She wondered why she resented the way in which her daughter-in-law talked about Russell. After all, what else could poor Lillian say? 'I'm getting too old to be rational. I even resented that good little Ann smoking in her own dining-room. If Russell were off my mind I should have nothing else to worry about. Which means, I suppose, that I should have nothing to live for,' she concluded, and went slowly down to watch all their faces: all that ecstasy of concern which at least children really have before they open their presents and find that they've got what they want.

Presents were given in the drawing-room, which was panelled and decorated with plaster swags and pilasters; with a pair of chandeliers, and heavily draped crimson curtains – too old and too rotted with dust and the sun ever to be moved. Now it was tricked out with holly and red *crêpe*-paper bells; wavering strands of tinsel trembled from the chandeliers; mistletoe, which made Vanessa think of very pale wicked people, was clustered in witch-like bunches. At the end of the room stood the Christmas-tree, creaking faintly under its weight of jewelled regalia. Down the centre of the room stood a row of the dining-room chairs, piled, loaded, hung, with each person's presents. The most charming surprise about Ann, thought her mother-in-law, as she stood watching the scene, was the thorough, lovely attention she gave to the enhancing of all these ceremonies. Looking at her, she seemed a small colourless creature, without the imagination or vitality for such effects. 'Nobody could arrange it all better!' she exclaimed, and saw Ann's quick burning little blush scorch over her face. 'Anyone can do it,' she said hastily; 'Lillian always has wonderful ideas when she's here.'

Donald moved towards her; there was something protective in his movement, his mother noticed. 'You maintain the standard,' he said, 'anyone can cut a dash.' He sounded almost conciliating, and Ann did not reply.

The gong was rung for the children. They had been waiting for it: their distinct clamour swelled – they rushed into the room on a tidal wave of anticipation.

The sights to see! It was not only their faces. Roddy, with a quick furtive look round the room first, taking out his painful plate, and dropping it into an empty flower-vase before he got down to his presents. Desmond, with the knife he had had in his stocking, hacking through the string on all his parcels before he opened one. Janet, still nearly a baby, shrieking with rage when the yellow tissue-paper was taken off her first present, wanting only to plunge her hands in and out of the lovely crackling colour, not understanding about presents at all. James, picking up each parcel and shaking it with nervous ravished little movements to find his train. Vanessa, gripping the back of her chair and staring passionately down at her pile, almost as though their wrappings were transparent, and she knew what lay before her. 'Do you want scissors, Vanessa?' called Ann, and Van's face flashed at once to that expression of blank docility which her aunt found impenetrable. 'No. thank you, Aunt Ann,' and she picked up the smaller parcel and carefully unpicked the ribbon.

She won't open my present yet, thought her grandmother, and turned to watch the amazing variety of gratitude which had begun to explode throughout the room. James raced through his other presents with gabbled thanks until he found his train, and retired to a corner with it. Roddy, who had been given a tricycle, rode madly round and round in the minimum circle shouting, 'Watch him riding: *watch him riding!*' Janet took one look at a white monkey Marie-Laure had unwrapped for her and burst into tears of terror and dislike. Donald had given Ann some garnets, but before she could put them on, Desmond seized his father for help with Meccano, and Ann had rushed to save the monkey situation with Janet.

Vanessa had reached the doll. Her grandmother watched her fingers – slow – almost clumsy with the ribbon, the lid of the box, the paper: then for a moment Vanessa was obscured from her by Marie-Laure thanking her for the pretty handkerchiefs. She heard Ann kindly admiring the doll, but no reply; and when she could see Vanessa again her present was still in its box: Vanessa, not touching it, had gone absolutely white. 'Gran made all her clothes,' Ann was saying; 'take her out, Vanessa, and see.' With a jerk Vanessa tore her eyes from the doll to her aunt – a trapped look, almost of hatred – before she lifted it out of the box. 'Ann doesn't understand,' thought her mother-in-law; 'I know. I can remember when I was ten, and they gave me a puppy. I couldn't speak: I thought I was going to die of my delight.'

Her aunt bent down and murmured something in Vanessa's ear. The little girl nodded without expression, and began picking her way across the room to her grandmother. Somehow, in spite of the short biscuit-coloured organdie with puff sleeves and a lace collar, in spite of her spindle legs with short white socks and her bony arms clutching the golden gorgeous doll, there was something wrong about her ...

'Thank you very much indeed for the beautiful present.'

She was still very pale. Her grandmother said gently: 'I'm so glad you like her. She hasn't got a name, so you must think of one.' And Vanessa answered immediately:

'Not now.' There was a pause, and then she added with a stiff social smile: 'Of course, I shall have to think.'

'But thank you,' she repeated, backing away.

'Why don't you take her upstairs?' suggested her grandmother, and Vanessa, in an unnaturally clear voice, cried, 'What a good idea!' and went.

She sounded exactly as though I was the child – as though she was humouring me, thought her grandmother.

'I think she *is* pleased, really,' said Ann. 'I know she wanted a doll very badly.'

'Heavens!' thought her mother-in-law; 'is *everyone* going to treat me as though I were nine?' Aloud, she said, 'I know exactly what Vanessa was feeling.'

When, a short while later, the telephone rang, it was Donald who answered it. 'If it's the Stevenses, ask them to tea *tomorrow*,' called Ann. 'Shut the door after your father, Desmond, or he won't hear a word with all our racket.'

Eventually – he returned. His mother looked up as he shut the door, and knew at once: her heart dropped with a single, sickening thud, as she rose slowly to her feet.

'You were ages: *was* it the Stevenses?' asked Ann, and then she saw his face.

'Mind! You're spoiling my accident, Uncle Donald. There's going to be the most enormous *awful* accident in a minute, and you're in the way!'

'Sorry, James.'

'Was that Mamma on the telephone?'

Donald answered easily. 'Yes. She sent you her love.'

'Ho! Van will be furious. She likes her love properly sent. Now everybody watch the great accident!'

But all the grown-ups had disappeared, except Marie-Laure. He had died about an hour ago, Donald told his mother and Ann. Lillian said that he'd had a stroke early in the morning, and he'd never regained consciousness. Ann's eyes filled with sudden, easy tears, but his mother sat still in her chair without a word.

'I said I'd go up at once to – to help – or do anything, but she wouldn't let me. She said she'd be down here in a couple of days, and that the doctor was being helpful and kind. She said please don't ring her up – she'll telephone when she's coming down.' He made a helpless gesture with his hands. 'I couldn't *argue* with her: she sounded pretty shocked; as though telling me at all was the most she could manage.'

Ann said: 'What about the children?'

'She said she left that to us. We were to tell Vanessa that she was coming down, anyway.'

'And where is my son to be buried? What about his funeral?'

Donald noticed with alarm that his mother was tearless.

Drumming her fingers on the arm of her chair, she repeated, 'What about my son's funeral?'

Before he could reply, the door burst open and Vanessa shot into the room. She wore a thick white jersey over her party frock and outdoor shoes covered with fresh mud. She rushed at Donald:

'She rang up! My *mother* rang up and you never called me! I've been waiting for her all day and you never called me!' Unable to bear her own agony of reproach, she dropped her face in her hands and burst into bitter tears.

Ann moved towards her, but she flung out an arm with a gesture absolutely denying comfort. 'You promised! I made you all promise that I could speak to her and then you never told me! How could you! How could you be so wickedly unfair!'

Donald, utterly taken aback, floundered: 'Look here, we've just had some bad news, you know, one thing at a time,' and then realized too late that she was only a child. They heard her draw in her breath with a little gasping sigh; an expression of fear, terrible, and terribly familiar to her face crept upon it; she clutched the wrist weighed down with the absurdly large watch, and then turned speechlessly to her grandmother, who had not moved or spoken.

'Your father is dead, Vanessa. Your mother is perfectly well. She is coming down here very soon. Very soon.'

Ann put Vanessa to bed and her mother-in-law on a sofa in her own sitting-room. She gave her children their Christmas tea, packed Donald off to drive Marie-Laure to her church, herded the children upstairs for their final rioting, cleared up the drawing-room and arranged that she and Donald should sup quietly in there.

Then, with a certain trepidation, she went up to see her mother-in-law.

She discovered her lying on her sofa with Vanessa in her dressing-gown sitting on a small beaded stool at her feet.

They were both sticking cloves into oranges and talking quietly.

'... evenly, but not too close together, because the orange will shrink as it dies and there must be room for the cloves. Ah! Ann, my dear. Vanessa is not being naughty: I sent for her, and when her orange is finished I shall send her back to bed.'

'Good.' Ann smiled uncertainly and Vanessa smiled gravely back. 'I really came to ask where you would like to dine?'

'I shall not come down again tonight. Change into your pretty clothes and have a quiet dinner with Donald which you richly deserve. Don't forget to wear your garnets. He would notice that, I think.'

Ann pulled the necklace out from under her jersey.

'I never took them off. I'd better go and dress up to them. Good night, Vanessa. I'll come and see you in bed.'

When Donald went up to their bedroom, he found her bathed, decorated with his necklace and dressed in the only dinner-dress he had ever admitted to liking.

'You *do* look nice: what a pretty dress too!' Then they both smiled at the old joke of the old dress.

'We are dining alone. I've got the children to bottle down, and you take your Mamma some sherry.'

'Is she all right?'

'She seems perfectly calm. She has remarkable courage. She was talking to Vanessa when I saw her – she's much better at that than I.'

'Oh – that reminds me. That wretched dog was bounding about the drive with this.' He held out the golden doll.

'Oh no! How did he get hold of it? *Covered* with mud. Oh, poor little Vanessa – she really hasn't had any luck today.'

'Looks as though he tried to bury it – of course his mouth is like silk – he hasn't bitten it anywhere. I've shut him up, but what shall we do about Vanessa?'

She put the doll on the stool. 'All her clothes will have to be washed, and her hair, and most of the doll, but I think she'll be all right. I'll do it tonight and put her by Vanessa's bed for the morning.'

On a sudden impulse he took her hand and kissed it, 'How exceedingly kind you are – darling Ann!'

Her face burned: she could not remember his ever kissing her hand before. She said, 'I always thought that kindness was a difficult thing to admire.'

With an unexpected grace of perception he replied, 'If kindness were your only quality, I might not admire it so much.'

To Donald, his mother said:

'If one has mourned someone's life as I have Russell's – for so long – their death is, I think, more of a shock than a grief, and I had not realized until today how very much Russell has lived at other people's expense. The expense to Vanessa, for example, has been too great.'

'Surely more to Lillian than anyone else!'

'Oh, infinitely more to her. But Lillian has the capacity – as Russell had – of inspiring such marked devotion, that I think she will find it again.'

She held out her glass to her son. 'Unlike you and me, my dear. We are the devoted. Do not forget that, or try to change it. It will be the constitution of your happiness, as it has been of mine.'

To Vanessa, she had said, 'I want to talk to you about your Mamma, as I know you love her very much. Perhaps people are put next to one another like beads. Look.' She unclasped her necklace of crystals and laid it on Vanessa's lap. 'That's you: and next to you, because you love her, your mother. And next to your mother because she loved him, your father. You see? Everybody needs one person and is also needed by someone else. Now your father dying means that the string has broken just there next to your mother and she will be very sad, so you must be very thoughtful about your love.'

'What was on the other side of my father?' Vanessa touched the spot with her finger. 'That bead?'

'I was there. That is the end of that end of the necklace. You see, your grandfather was on the other side of me.'

Vanessa looked up solemnly. 'I see.' There was a brief silence, then she asked hesitantly: 'And the other side of me?'

'What about James? He's much smaller than you. He needs someone.' She smiled and joined the ends together. 'Or you can do that, and then I am next to you. You may keep the necklace. Run along.'

Alone, she indulged in no philosophy, reflecting, a little wearily, that it was very much easier to comfort other people than oneself. Her son was dead, and she was not comforted, until before she finally slept, she remembered how, when she had mentioned Alec, Vanessa had looked up, her hair scraped back from her eggshell forehead, and in her eyes – Russell's eyes – a look of ageless, silent compassion.

When James returned from his bath he found Vanessa already in bed.

'Where have you been?'

'To see Gran.'

'You weren't at tea either,' he accused. 'A piece of cake has been saved for you. With the H of Happy *and* the I out of Christmas. Lucky swipe!'

She opened her mouth to tell him not to call people swipes and shut it again. He had been scarlet with over-excitement and now he looked belligerent and near to tears. His train was arranged on two chairs by his bed.

'Did you show Mrs Bond your train?'

'I showed her. She just said "Fancy". She says that whatever you show her,' he replied gloomily. 'But I told her Dad was dead just when I left. She didn't say "Fancy" then.'

'What did she say?'

'Nothing. She gave a sort of raspberry gasp, and then she told Ruby to turn the Light Programme off.' He got into bed.

'James – are you sad about it? About Dad, I mean.'

He looked blank. 'I haven't thought properly yet. It is a difficult thing to think about, isn't it? Are you? Do you want to do some crying? Can I have your watch?'

'I've stopped crying: I'm too old for it.' He looked so hurt that she added, 'But you can wear my watch for the night.' She got out of bed and strapped it sloppily round his wrist. He looked at it with satisfaction and seized his train.

'Listen. The train is going to run ...' He looked up at her and casually gave her a splendid kiss.

When she was back in bed he said: 'Van! Dad – I suppose now ... he's just a holy ghost?'

She turned to him, a little startled. He was furiously winding-up his train.

'He might be, James. I don't know. Ask tomorrow.'

'Turn off the light. This train is going to run in the dark.'

He held it up whirring. 'I would have liked to show it to Dad.'

The clockwork noise ran slowly down – coughed and was silent. James said:

'That's the very end of Christmas.'

'WALKING out on her in the middle of the night! I'm not easily shocked, but that shocks me!'

His conversation, she thought, was full of exceptions he made to his own rules. 'They've only been married a few weeks – it's just a tiff.'

'I dare say.' He stretched out a sunburned muscular arm, reached for a ginger-nut and popped it whole into his mouth. Speaking through it, he went on: 'But he's got his own way out of it, hasn't he? It's he who's off to Scotland, spoiling her holiday and leaving her on her own. Poor little thing! She's only eighteen – only a child!'

'Shirley won't be on her own: she's coming down to us just the same.'

He said nothing for a moment, swilled back the rest of his chestnut-coloured tea, wiped his moustache with a huge, navy handkerchief, and thrusting it back into his breeches pocket pronounced, 'Well! It may sound funny to you, but *I* don't like the idea of *my* daughter being mucked about. It annoys me, that's all. Gets my goat.'

There was silence in the kitchen while Kate Ewbank did not retort, 'She's my daughter too, isn't she? How do you know she's being mucked about?' or simply, 'You don't say!' Years of not airing them had cramped and damped her responses into this kind of thing which she would not sink to out loud.

The stable clock struck five and Brian Ewbank got to his feet, collecting his old tweed jacket from the back of his chair. Then, stooping slightly to see himself in it, he combed his thick, wavy grey hair in front of the small mirror that hung by the sink. 'You'll be fetching her from the station, then?'

'I will.'

The Ewbanks lived in what had been the coachman's cottage near a large Victorian stable block built round three sides of a courtyard. It had been designed to serve the huge neo-gothic house that was now a girls' boarding school set in vast, semi-derelict grounds of parkland and wooded drives. At five-thirty on summer term-time evenings he took a flock of girls, chiefly called Sarah and Caroline, on bulging, grass-fed ponies for a ride. They called him Brian behind his back, but he was really Captain Ewbank, and they held interminable conferences about whether his marriage was happy, or a tragic failure.

The moment Kate was alone, Marty, the tortoise-shell cat, slammed through the cat door with a mouse in her jaws. She tossed it under a chair, mentioned it several times in a high-pitched voice until she had forced Kate to meet her glassy, insolent gaze, and then began to crunch it up like a club sandwich. She liked Kate, in a limited way, to share her triumphs. In ten seconds the mouse was gone, she had drunk a saucer of milk and was polishing her spotless paws. She kept herself in a gleaming state of perpetual readiness – like a fire engine.

When she had cleared the tea, Kate went up to make the bed in Shirley's old room, in case she would rather sleep there than in the twin beds pushed together to make a double in the spare room. She also moved the jar of marigolds and pinks. She wanted Shirley to feel welcome. After that, she could not think at all what else she ought to do, and stood motionless, wondering what it could possibly be. But then, as sometimes nowadays, a moment after she had stopped physically moving and was still, despair engulfed her, as dense, as sudden and palpable as stepping into a rain-cloud or a fog. Senses of futility and failure fused; then the pall receded, leaving her with a feeling of weakness and mediocrity.

Percy was calling from his room, which was downstairs by the front door. Whenever she thought of him, she had to pull herself together. 'You still have your health,' she told herself. Apart from a touch of arthritis, migraines that irregularly punctured her attempts to face up to things, and these freakish sweats – hot flushes by name and as amusing to those unencumbered by them as piles or gout – she had little to complain about, whereas poor old Percy ...

He had somehow got wind of the fact that she was going out in the car; must have heard Brian mentioning the station, although goodness knows he was deaf enough when he felt like it. By the time she got to him, he had levered himself to his feet with one hand perilously heavy on the corner of his loaded card-table. He had always borne a marked resemblance to Boris Karloff, and since his – fortunately mild – stroke now looked astonishingly like that actor in the role of Frankenstein's Monster. He'd got his speech painfully back, but he kept it to a minimum.

'I'm only going to fetch Shirley from the station, Father.'

'Shoes,' he said, his hopeful smile undimmed. 'Outdoor shoes.' He pointed with his stick to where his black shoes – as sleek and polished as a pair of police cars – were parked beneath his wardrobe. But his gesture with the stick involved further weight upon the card-table; it tipped, and its formidable coverage fell and rolled all over the floor as he lurched involuntarily on to his bed in a sitting position.

'Whoops-a-daisy,' he said, smiling again to show he was all right, and stuck one of his dreadful old feet with its Walt Disney ogre's toenails almost into her face as she knelt recovering his travelling clock, his pills, his spilled water-carafe, his spectacles, his address book that he kept up to date by crossing off his friends as they died, his saucer that he'd used for grape pips, a couple of chessmen he'd been mending and a plastic heart-shaped box in which he kept alternate rows of false teeth at night.

'Percy, dear, there isn't time: I'll be late. I won't be long.'

His lower lip trembled ponderously, like a baby's, working up to a scene; he withdrew his foot, and then, with a look so cunning that it was pathetic, shot the other one out at her.

'Oh – all *right* then,' she said, and fetched his socks.

In the tack room, Eunice, the stable-girl, was applying mascara to the double pair of false eyelashes that were her second most salient feature. Brian knew that she had heard him come in, but he also knew what he thought she liked. Coming up behind her, he put a large hand over each heavily confined breast, and squeezed them like someone tooting a horn. She squealed.

'Bry – *yern*!'

'I'll be a bit late tonight. Mind you wait.'

She did not answer, but he knew she would.

In the train from Manchester to London, Shirley decided over and over again that her marriage was a total, utter, flop. It must be, if in just over eight weeks they could have a row like that. After he had gone off ('Please yourself!') – what a filthy, *stupid, childish* thing to say! – she had never cried so much before in her life; in fact she couldn't believe he'd only been gone twenty minutes, as she discovered he had when she went to wash her face and happened to look at her watch. She'd cleared up the kitchen with meticulous care, wasn't going to let him put her in the wrong about a wife's mess in the flat, but she'd thrown away the sausage rolls so that he wouldn't have anything to eat when he came back – serve him right. But he hadn't *come* back. Instead, when she was frantic with waiting and wanting to tell him what she thought of him, he'd rung to say he was staying the night with friends. She'd been icy on the telephone, but the moment she'd rung off, she'd burst into tears again. Then, like a fool, she'd waited to see him in the morning, but he still didn't come back, and she'd missed the express and had to catch a slow train. It was a failure all right.

By the time she'd changed stations in London and caught the four-twenty from Charing Cross, her whole life with him had begun to seem faintly unreal. She hated the flat, she hated Manchester – she didn't know a single person there, she missed the country, she hated the housework and the awful, endless business of shopping for boring petty things, getting food ready and clearing it up. None of it had turned out at all as she had imagined. Beforehand, she'd thought of being married as candlelit dinners, friends dropping in, using all the presents, setting the table as perfectly as she did her face, moving in the television world (Douglas was a cameraman), Douglas's friends admiring her, envying him, sometimes even making him a little jealous ... they'd bring her flowers and chocs and ask her advice about their girlfriends. None of this had happened at all. Instead, he'd come back at awful hours – never the same time – fagged out, only talking about his work and a whole lot of people she never met; when she wasn't bored, she was lonely. She missed her friends and her life at home and Dad who'd always been so decent to her ...

As they changed into their riding clothes, Sarah Hughenden said to Caroline Polsden-Lacey, 'I tell you one thing. He's got the most super heavenly sweat.'

'Who?'

'Brian – stupid. He smells of smoked salmon.'

'How do you know?'

'I sort of fell up against him.'

'Sarah! You really *are*!'

It took Kate nearly half an hour to get her father dressed and into the car. In spite of her telling him it was a hot day, he wore a vest, flannel shirt, thick Norfolk jacket, his burberry and a cashmere muffler she'd given him last Christmas. He also took his pocket book of British birds in case a British bird got near enough – and stayed still long enough – for him to identify it. It was indeed hot. The wild roses were blanched by the heat; buttercups glittered in the rich grass, the chestnut trees lining the unkempt drive had leaves that were already shabby from drought, and the Herefords clumped together under them in a miasma of flies. Without glancing at him, Kate could feel the intensity with which her father was looking out of the car window; she was unhappily divided between going slowly to give him the maximum enjoyment, and not being late for Shirley, who would anyway not be pleased at his making a third in the car. It was extraordinary, she felt, how much of life consisted of having to displease somebody.

As Shirley walked down the platform, she could see her mother standing at the barrier, dressed, as usual, in a faded flowered cotton skirt, a blue tee-shirt and sandals, her dark glasses pushed up over her fringe. From the distance, she looked like a dowdy, rather arty girl. At least, Shirley thought, I've stopped her wearing trousers – she really wasn't the shape for them.

They kissed, rather awkwardly; neither was sure what degree of warmth was appropriate to the occasion. Kate said quickly,

'I'm terribly sorry, but I simply had to bring Percy.'

'Surely you didn't *have* to.'

'You know how he feels about going out in the car. How are you?' She looked at her daughter's incredibly pretty, apparently unravaged face, turning sulky now at the news about her grandfather.

'I'm all right,' stony, snubbing, walking ahead of her mother in silence to the car.

Percy was dragging a dusty fruit-drop from his overcoat pocket. He had recently taken to eating them with the cellophane wrappers still on, and enjoyed being asked why he did so, so that he could say he always ate his sweet papers. He longed to confound people by turning out always to have done something that surprised them. He popped the sweet in just as they got into the car, but when neither of them asked him, he took the sweet out again, dropped it on the floor and ground his foot on it as though it was a cigarette.

'Here's Shirley,' said Kate, pretending not to notice.

'So I see. Had a good term?'

'She hasn't been to school, Father. She's been in Manchester, with Douglas.'

He crunched his dentures and didn't answer. Kate thought he was sulking because he'd got something wrong, but really he was peeved because he hadn't embarrassed Shirley with his pretended memory lapse (he knew she wasn't at school, and who on earth was Douglas?).

'How's my father?'

'He's fine. He's taking the evening ride.'

'What's the new stable-girl like?'

'I've hardly seen her. She's called Eunice.'

'Is she attractive?'

Kate paused before replying evenly: 'Oh yes, I should think she's quite attractive.' It had recently begun to amaze her that in all these years, Shirley had never noticed anything ...

'... and I'm not a child! Why should he suddenly spoil all our plans just because he wants to work on his wretched film! If he can't be bothered even to think what I might feel, why on earth did he ever want to marry me?' She was sitting cross-legged on the floor of her room, having a post-cry cigarette, and looking, Kate thought, very childish indeed.

'Perhaps he *had* to do the job?' she suggested – very gently, but not gently enough.

'Whenever I try to tell you anything, you always take the other person's side! You *always* do!'

'I didn't mean it to sound like that: I'm only trying to understand. I can't believe he simply wanted to hurt your feelings.'

'He doesn't care about my feelings. All he cares about is his bloody film unit. He never stops thinking and talking about them.'

'Could you have gone to Scotland with him?'

'He never said so. Anyway, I've told him it's not my idea of a holiday to sit about cooped up in some ghastly hotel while he's out on an oil rig or something. He told me he'd got three days' leave, and he promised to come home. He *promised* me.' She thrust her knuckles under her firm little chin and glared into space. After a minute, she said:

'The truth is, it's got to be all or nothing for me. I'm jealous of his work.' She looked at her mother with something like triumph. 'That's what it is! I expect him to put me first, and he doesn't, and it makes me jealous!'

The discovery seemed actually to relieve her. After it, she became much easier to reason with: allowed Kate to discuss with her the possibility of getting some sort of part-time job, admitted that Douglas had said something about standing in for a friend whose wife was having a baby, and even volunteered that she could be terrible when she didn't get her own way. She was of an age, Kate thought, when self-recrimination seemed to be unaccompanied by pain. 'I know I've got a hot temper!' She was simply very young for a situation into which her appearance had trapped her so early; an only and childish child, which Kate, in her turn, had to admit meant that she was to some degree spoiled, although with Brian as a father, how could she have prevented it? He had always defended her, backed her up whatever she did ...

'Where's the most beautiful girl in the world?'

He was standing at the bottom of the staircase, and Kate, in the kitchen doorway, watched her as she stood at the top – dressed now in her old jeans and a sleeveless green angora jerkin: she posed for a moment, and then hurled herself down – hair flying, eyes shining – into his arms. He gave a great laugh, and held her at arm's length.

'Let's look at you. *Mrs* Thornton: let's have a look.'

'I'm fine, Daddy.' But Kate could hear that little touch of the gallant waif – knew that those dog-violet eyes were gazing at her father with the expression of quivering self-reliance that he would find irresistible. Was she play-acting, or was it real? Certainly their relationship was like the way fathers and daughters went on in bad films: even in these few weeks she had forgotten how much and how quickly it exasperated her.

'Mrs Thornton!' He had picked up her left hand now, and was contemplating the gold wedding ring quizzically. 'To think I should live to see the day! I tell you one thing. I'm jealous of Mr Thornton.'

'You needn't be. Oh – you smell – *nice!*'

Kate was conscious of a small, but regular, hammer thudding from somewhere inside her as she became miserably transfixed.

'And what, may I ask, does this call itself? He caressed the fluffy green jerkin that seemed to be fastened only in one place just below her breasts, so that the sides flew out to reveal the slender rib cage, tiny waist and concave upper belly.

'Really, Daddy – you are impossible! Your own daughter!' Some luxuriant head-tossing, and his hairy wrists picked from the sides of her jeans.

'How do you get your hair to shine like that!'

'My herbal rinse.' Demure now, walking towards her, ahead of him, into the kitchen.

('How dare you behave like this! – In front of your wife! Behind your husband's back!') She needed two voices to scream it, but her body felt like some roaring conduit of surging blood, with a trap-door slammed shut in the bottom of her throat. As they approached her, she began fiddling unsteadily with the strawberries in the colander before her.

'Oh – strawberries! How fabulous!' Kate recognized the stringing-along-with-Mummy tone that so often came after what had gone before.

'Don't bother your mother now, she's busy, and I'm going to take you for a drink at the Woodman.' His hole-in-one technique, she called that.

'Oh – great! Let's ride, Dad: we can ride through the wood and up the lane.'

A few minutes later, they were gone. There had been a

few last moments of 'Sure you don't want any help?' 'Sure you don't mind?' followed by 'We'll be back at half past on the dot – promise,' and then they were off. She was left alone in silence – except for the cold tap dripping and the distant, velvety gabble of Percy's radio.

She discovered that things were taking on a dirty, speckled appearance, and she fumbled in her bag to find the orange pills encased in foil that helped to prevent migraine. Cafergot had to be crunched up to work quickly, and she washed down the cheap, stale chocolate taste with a glass of tap water. She wanted a cigarette, but that would be fatal. What she must do was to sit quite still, and relax, but that only made it more difficult to stop what she had just been thinking. After trying for a bit, it seemed reasonable – even mild – simply to dislike them, compared with what she felt about herself.

They came back to supper in high spirits with half a bottle of gin. She didn't dare have a drink, but he made Shirley and himself a couple of John Collins with a tin of grapefruit juice and soda. Supper was cold, so it didn't matter when they had it, and she did Percy's tray while they finished their drinks. Brian was in his entertaining, expansive mood; taking off the little girls he taught to ride; 'Oh – Cuptain Ewbunk!' He was a good mimic – could do all the various off-white upper-class vowel sounds; could indicate the braces on their teeth, their stiff little pigtails below their hard velvet hats. He finished with a telling imitation of a fat and frightened girl being taught to jump. The sports mistress had many times told Kate how popular he was with the girls. And, of course, someone at the pub had thought Shirley was his girl-friend: Shirley thought that madly funny. She ate like a school-girl – three helpings of new potatoes and home-cooked tongue: 'It's so marvellous not cooking. I'm simply not the domesticated type, I've decided.' It wasn't until she returned from taking Percy his strawberries that she heard Brian say casually,

'There's no need for you to go back on Tuesday. Stay and

help me knock some sense into that new pony. He's not safe for the children and he's not up to my weight.'

And Shirley, seeing her mother, said automatically: 'Oh – I couldn't. I'll have to go back.'

'Why not? If you stay a little extra, you might also knock some sense into that husband of yours.'

Kate said: 'Brian! Of course she must go back.'

'I don't see that. He shouldn't go flouncing off – out all night – that's no way to treat any woman – let alone your wife. Do him good to worry about her for a change.'

Kate turned to her daughter: 'Shirley, you don't really feel that you can –'

But Shirley, pouring cream on to her strawberries, said quickly: 'I was talking to Dad in the pub about it. I thought it would be interesting to know what another man thought, you know –'

'Damn right! Well, I think the sooner he learns that life doesn't entirely revolve round his blasted television the better. I mean, he'd made a plan with Shirley, and he ought to have stuck to it, that's what he ought to have done. I mean, she's never going to know where she is, is she? One minute he makes a promise – the next minute he breaks it. That's no way to treat any girl – let alone my girl. Well?' Magnanimity was momentarily extended to her: 'What do you think?'

She took a long breath trying to control her anger at his outrageous attitude and said coldly, 'I think you should mind your own business.'

Before she had finished speaking, the telephone rang, and Shirley, glad of the escape, ran to answer it. A second later, she was back: 'It's Douglas. I'm going to take it upstairs. Will you put the receiver back for me?'

When she had done so, and returned to the kitchen determined to stop the irresponsible mischief he was making, Kate found him on his feet, cramming hunting flask, pipe and tobacco into his pockets; his face suffused, set sullen, avoiding her eye.

'I'm off. Forgot to fetch that liniment from the vet. The grey's been knocking herself. Forgot it earlier.'

'Don't bother to tell me a pack of –'

'Tell her not to wait up. I've promised her a ride in the morning.'

'Brian, listen to me. Don't you dare interfere any more with her marriage. It's not fair: it's very wrong.' It sounded weak as she said it, and he seized the advantage.

'*I'm* not interfering. She asked me what I thought, and I told her. That's natural, isn't it? She's only a child. And why should my opinion be any more interfering than yours? Tell me that.'

'You know perfectly well why it is. And she's no longer a child. She's a married woman.'

'I *don't* know. And I don't care. I do – not – care a bugger – what you think – about anything at all.'

He went, shutting, nearly slamming, the kitchen door behind him.

The telephone conversation seemed to be going on for ever. She supposed drearily that it must be a good sign they were talking at such length: she was sure Douglas cared. Poor boy, he was only twenty-two, had his way to make, and although he was reputed to be clever, cleverness was not particularly helpful when it came to making a marriage work – especially with someone as self-willed as Shirley. Could they, she and Brian, as parents, have stopped her marrying so young? If they had been united about it and had wanted to, she supposed they might just have – have made her wait longer, anyhow. But they were not united, and for different reasons neither of them had seen fit even to try. Brian had always thought that Shirley should have whatever she wanted, and she ... she was ashamed of her reason – it wasn't even a reason really, just a hope, forlorn as it had turned out, that Brian would be – easier, a bit nicer to her, if Shirley simply wasn't there.

Her head felt as though someone had bruised something inside it rather badly, but she decided not to take any more of the migraine drug. When she had finished clearing supper, she noticed Shirley's cigarettes, and took one for something to do.

She heard Shirley ring off, and minutes later she strolled into the kitchen, cool, expressionless, clearly pleased with herself.

'Where's Dad?'

'He's gone out – said don't wait up.'

'I wouldn't dream of going to bed yet. Whew! It's hot!' She sat on the corner of the table, kicked off her shoes and put her bare feet on the arm of her father's chair. Her toenails were painted a pale, pearly pink.

'Well – is everything better now?'

'Douglas? Oh – fine. He's coming down tomorrow.'

'Shirley, I am glad. How has he managed to get away?'

'Oh – some change in the shooting schedule – I didn't bother. The point is, I've won!'

Kate looked at her. 'How do you mean?'

She repeated impatiently, 'I've won! He wanted me to go back – to meet him at the flat, but I told him come down here or else.' She leaned across the table to take a cigarette.

'I took one, I hope you don't mind.'

'Feel free. Got a light?'

Kate struck a match and held it out, watching her daughter's face as she bent her head, cigarette poised in the wide Cupid's-bow mouth, heavy lashes lowered over the violet eyes, calmly intent upon her first puff.

'But he'll have to go back again on Monday night, won't he? It hardly seems worth it for such a little time.'

'He thinks it's worth it. Any case, he had no choice. Daddy was quite right. He'll think twice before he ever walks out on me again. I haven't even told him I'll go back with him for sure.'

'Shirley! You can't behave like this! You're just *playing* at being married! You can't be so –'

'I can! I can! I'm perfectly serious. He wants far more from me than I want from him. He's more turned on than I am. Let him sweat.'

There was a brutal pause, then she added with some feeling: 'I *hate* being alone. I *hate* that flat. I *loathe* being tied down. Daddy said I could stay as long as I like.'

Then, perhaps aware of some fractional discomfort from her mother's silence, she rose from the table and began looking for her shoes.

'Where's he gone to at this time of night?'

'To put some liniment on a horse.'

'In the stables?'

Kate hesitated only a moment: 'I expect in the stables.'

After she had gone, Kate remained completely still: why had she done it? But she refused to consider why – simply sat at the table and followed Shirley: down the garden path to the gate, along the drive to the archway; she might pause there to see if there was a light in the stables, but there would be no light since none was needed. Would she go on, as Kate had done that first time, long ago, because there had been an urgent telephone message? It had been autumn then, and dark, but some instinct had driven her to the stables door, undone at the latch and ajar. The horses had shifted softly in their straw; moonlight, like a shaft of lemonade, had lain across the little empty coal-grate in the tack room and the place had the affectionate, sweet smell of warm horses and hay. She had stood there wondering (where could he have gone?), when, with shocking suddenness, and from just above her head, had come a high-pitched, explosively ugly and frightening laugh. Dead silence: she had heard her own heart beating . . . then a man's inaudible protest and heavy, sibilant, thrashing commotion. They were in the hay-loft; she had turned to see the ladder set squarely to its open trap. The laughter had begun moaning and she had fled. Since that first time, she had returned once or twice when he had hired new girls, but only enough to feed her reason, to keep her fearful hatred sane, because she had known that if there was no reason for feeling as she did, she must be mad.

She had done nothing. Shirley had been determined to go – she had simply not prevented her.

She became aware of Percy calling. He might have been calling for some time; for once she had forgotten him, and she hurried, with a feeling of shame, to his room. She had got him undressed and into bed before his supper, but had not even fetched his supper tray, let alone settled him for the night.

He gave her his gentle lop-sided smile as she came in; he had been sticking things into his scrap-book and seemed not to have noticed the time. As soon as he saw her, he began hunting through the back pages.

'You haven't eaten your strawberries!'

He gave her a reproachful look. 'Too many stones.' He was still searching in his book. 'Here! Found Douglas. Douglas and Shirley marriage.' It was the wedding picture cut out of the local paper. 'Douglas,' he explained again, in case she wasn't sure.

'Yes,' she agreed. She helped him out of bed to the lavatory, and got his pillows right for the night. His sheets seemed always to be covered with toast crumbs. She filled up his water-carafe, opened his window and put the box for his false teeth handy. When he was in bed again, she bent to kiss his cold, papery-dry forehead and he closed his eyes as though for a benediction. She picked up the supper tray and was turning to go when he suddenly thrust a screwed-up piece of paper at her, pushing it into her hand as though he was stopping up a chink.

'For you. To read.'

'All right, Father dear.' He sometimes wrote lists of what he needed: glue, fruit-drops, aspirin – that kind of thing.

'Read later.'

'Yes. I will.'

In the kitchen, Shirley stood heating something on the stove. She must have heard her mother come in, but neither turned round nor spoke.

Kate said: 'You're back.' She had begun to feel afraid.

'So it would seem.' Hostility was naked. She poured the contents of the saucepan into a mug and turned off the heat.

'Why did you let me go to the stables? You knew what was going on, didn't you? What made you do that?'

Kate tried to say something, but she was not a liar, and could not.

'I suppose you thought it would turn me against him, and make me sorry for you! Well it hasn't. I suppose you thought that as you don't enjoy screwing, you'd put me off it! It's him I'm sorry for – having to go to those lengths. I despise you – more completely than I've ever despised anyone in my life! Letting me go out there was just typical of how horrible you really are. Drab, and smug and self-righteous. Underneath it – you're just nasty. Nobody could love you – not a single person in the world!' Her hand holding the milk was shaking, but she didn't spill any – just walked out of the room, shutting the kitchen door behind her.

Kate stood, heart hammering, listening to the steps going away from her to the bedroom above. She put up her hand, to hold her face together, and the piece of screwed-up paper fell on to the table. When she smoothed it out the note, written large and quavering with a black felt pen, read: 'Thank you, my Darling, for the Lovely Outing in your Motor Car. Today.'

She read it for a long time. The message, with its drops of grateful love, made a slow, unsteady course, until eventually, in the end, it reached her.

TOUTES DIRECTIONS

'*Must* you go?' they said at intervals. They said it often enough for it to cease seeming like a rhetorical question. In fact, it was, and always had been, but each refusal from Harriet strengthened their, or rather Mrs Mouncey's, theoretical hospitality.

The villa had new guests pending; from England, America and Italy. They were all the kind of people that Mrs Mouncey was glad, afterwards, to have had. She mixed or alternated them with a few of the wild, incomprehensible young, who were the sons and daughters of other famous international acquaintances. Mrs Mouncey had no friends, which she equated in her mind with broad-mindedness. She did not in the *least* want Harriet to stay. The girl had not been a 'success', although she had the kind of prim beauty that put her in some unknown category – certainly not the 'you can't take your eyes off her' class, but she was not 'good fun' either. Harriet had been explained simply as the goddaughter of a long-dead friend, Lady Stanhope. This served Mrs Mouncey very well, putting her into a vague but kindly light which she seemed so often to be behind, or beyond.

Harriet's manners were that of the perfect, passive guest. She seemed to have no particular, tiresome requirements – like wishing to shop in Cannes, or sight-see, or indeed do anything at all. She bathed obediently at the ordered times, she sun-bathed, but judiciously – her skin was the kind that went with copper-coloured hair. She drank Campari sodas, Paradis, Pernod, or Cinzano of any colour. She looked good in a bikini, and changed in the evenings into Liberty voiles: washable and uncrushable described far more of her in these circumstances than Mrs Mouncey knew.

She had always been going on Friday, in a train along the

coast, to spend one night with her friend, Susan Cole, who had a villa inland of Marseille. 'A friend' she had simply explained as a girl whom she had gone through college with in America. Mrs Mouncey, who did not like to waste a moment of her worthless time, embraced her wearing an aquamarine *peignoir* beneath which her corsets felt like a salad basket, and also equipped with an enormous amount of Femme and some oil on her face that had none of the unobtrusiveness that those embracing her might have hoped for. However, she sent her maid to pack Harriet's cheap suitcase, and her chauffeur to the little railway station that looked like a millionaire's child's toy, with its small, neatly placed palms, its clean and empty ticket-office, its hanging baskets of bright pink geraniums, and its glaring white platform. The sky was perfectly and entirely blue, the railway track like the back of a blue-bottle. The chauffeur, who was French, put her case on the edge of the platform and stood as though he was waiting for something. Harriet told him haltingly not to stay (her French was almost nil) and then, after he had gone, wondered whether she ought to have tipped him. Life at Cap Ferrat had been fraught with these problems. Anyway, she hadn't, she pointed out to herself, and this made her look in her pocket-book. She had enough for her second-class train fare back to England, and a hundred francs plus some small change that she had difficulty in sorting out. An official put in an appearance at the ticket-office, so she was able to buy her *billet*. The train was coming. There was nobody else on the platform at all, and when the little train came puffing round the bend, it seemed to Harriet as though only the sight of her stopped it. She opened the nearest coach door, and dragged her suitcase in. She wore a cream linen suit with a dark brown shirt, and as soon as she was in the train, took the jacket off. She was too hot, and she still felt Mrs Mouncey's oil and Femme on her face. She wore her hair with a centre parting and coiled round her neck. This was also too hot, but she had not felt equal to leaving the villa with her hair down or plaited. One of the

most extraordinary weeks of her life, she decided, and at
once began to imagine telling Sue about it all, while they sat
in Sue's kitchen, or the village restaurant. She had never
seen Sue's house, and as Sue hardly ever came to England,
and Harriet could hardly ever afford to leave it, their com-
munication had been confined to letters in which Susan's
writing had never changed from the bold upright script
taught to rich girls in America, although her sentences were
childishly short and assumed in Harriet a knowledge of
French village life that Harriet certainly had not got. She
had left America earlier than Sue, and had sent herself to an
art school in London. She got into it easily enough, but it
took her three years to discover that she was not, and never
would be, the kind of painter that she had always imagined
herself becoming. By the time she reached this point, the
legacy was spent, and ever since she had had to do one
boring thing after another for a living, until a very charming middle-aged interior decorator had invited her to help
him with colour schemes for those clients who had no views
on this matter excepting what they didn't like, which was
practically everything. Harriet had an excellent sense of
colour (this capacity had been a main part of the trap that
had sprung her into art school). But she had also a wonderfully calm, apparently passive approach to people; the clients
loved her, since she made it so easy for them to say that they
had thought of, bought and collected everything for themselves. Mr Crane had been delighted with her, and he and
Rudolph had both decided that she was the perfect link with
difficult clients. So, more money after two years, and time to
save up for a holiday, until Mrs Mouncey, looking for some
fabric to stick on the walls of her downstairs john, had encountered her, uncovered the tenuous link with 'poor Meg
Stanhope' and invited her for a free week in her villa at Cap
Ferrat. Harriet had accepted with a sense of excitement;
some mirages turn out to be real, after all, but loyalty and
curiosity compelled her to combine this holiday with a visit
to Sue. It was then that she realized that Sue had never in-

vited her to her home, although she had written an ecstatic and ill-spelt reply to Harriet's letter inviting herself.

The week in the villa had turned into a luxury nightmare: one of the gardeners had climbed through her window one night and actually tried to go to bed with her. It was not that Harriet was against going to bed with gardeners; she was miserably and chronically tied to an architect who was married with four children, and before going to France she had promised herself – and, far worse, him – that she would remain constant to their furtive, irregular, and increasingly unsatisfactory hours of meeting. But other difficulties at the villa had proved more constant than the gardener, who had actually looked very nice, with black hair, brandy-snap eyes and white, or gold, teeth regularly disposed within his inviting smile. He had given up with all the good-humour of an experienced optimist. No, it was the prolonged drinks time, twice a day, when people talked almost exclusively of other people whom they knew and Harriet did not. If they had talked about literature, painting, or even music, she would have been able to keep her end up, but when they were not bandying about one might almost say geographical names, they were immersed in stock markets of Wall Street and the City, with American politics, with where they had just been and where they were just going. Their clothes, their cars, their hair, their air was of such palatial well-being that they might have come from Mars. She also could not understand their jokes, and there is little more frightening than that. At any rate, she gradually became afraid of them, and this, with Harriet, meant that she never spoke unless spoken to, did everything she could to do as everybody else did, but was so passive and reserved that nobody made her, and she was finally pronounced frigid and dull by the men and odd and difficult by the women. Everybody concluded these remarks with the coda that she had 'good manners'.

Anyway, she could tell Sue all about it, and they would add some new jokes to the very old but private ones that were beginning to wear out.

The train stopped many times: people got in and out at the next station. None of *them* were rich. One man put two live ducks, their legs tied together, on to the rack. The ducks were silent with fright, and the air smelled of hot feathers. An old lady, blackly dressed, came into Harriet's compartment with a very young olive-skinned girl carrying a baby. Harriet was unable to understand whether they were speaking French, but when the baby began to cry, the girl muttered something to her mother and began to undo her blouse, whereupon the grandmother whipped off her black woollen shawl and held it round mother and baby as a tent, or shield from Harriet's eyes. This was more like travelling, Harriet thought to herself in order not to feel bored. The moment that daughter, grandmother and baby got in, she had a passionate desire to smoke, but felt that this would be wrong. She stared out of the window as the apricot, blue, pink, white and even unpainted houses or villas with their palms, their oleander, their bougainvillaea, their geraniums and washing hanging from lines passed slowly by. Their shutters were nearly all closed, as of houses asleep. There seemed to be no birds, but when the train stopped, she could hear the tireless, insistent cicadas. Sometimes the sea was visible, purple blue or swimming-bath green with huge coloured parasols that looked perfect on the pale sand. She imagined all the people she had left, having long siestas before bathing again, having drinks, and playing *boule* on the gravel outside the front door (the chauffeur had to move all the cars for this every day). Thinking of this, she, too, fell into a light sleep.

She awoke suddenly, sure that this must be her station, and it was. She struggled to haul her suitcase off the rack, convinced in a sleepy panic that the train would move on before she could get out. But nothing was like that: a porter opened the door for her, and took her case. At the end of the long city platform she could see Sue standing, in dark glasses, jeans and a sleeveless shirt. What she had always worn, thought Harriet with a pang of affection. Her hair was still short and cut with a fringe. She had not yet seen Harriet, so a moment of the most acute observation was open to her – restricted only by distance. When she felt that she could learn no more, she waved, and instantly Sue waved back at twice the speed. They met, hugged each other and laughed, and each thought – quite wrongly – that the other had not changed. Each was so charged with things to tell and to say, that they said nothing, until the porter had brought Harriet's bag to the car, and Sue had thanked and tipped him so that he went off smiling.

Sue unlocked the car, shoved Harriet's bag in the boot, and then motioned her to sit in front. In a moment they were hooting and grinding their way out of Marseille. Susan, who had driven since she was ten, and in a number of countries at that, swerved, hooted, halted her way through the town at maximum speed, and such, Harriet felt, must be her concentration, that they exchanged no more than 'Journey all right?' 'Fine, it was a real neat little train.' It had begun in their letters to each other: the practice of using the most outrageously appropriate English or American phrases; on the whole, American from Harriet and English from Sue, although occasionally both slipped up.

Out of Marseille, they started the gradual climb up to Sue's village. The air began to smell of hot rosemary and thyme: the sun was setting as slowly and majestically as possible: furnace clouds, tipped with gold, and backed by a sky that was now the colour of lavender. Their silence in the town seemed to have made spontaneous talk between them either to have got lost, or never to have existed at all. Harriet (contrary to all her imagining) was just about to announce that she had been involved with Tim for two years, and to go on from there – should she leave him or should she not: she was really very tired of carrying the burden of his guilt and self-pity – when Sue suddenly said, 'I'm pregnant. Jesus! I'm sorry it had to be tonight.'

'How do you mean?'

'I mean, ducks, that I've got to do something about it tonight. If I'd known, I would have called you at your ritzy villa and tried to put you off.'

'But why on earth should you have done that?'

'Because I thought that *you* would think we'd have a lovely cosy evening eating and talking about old, hard times. I'm truly sorry.'

There was a really dead silence. Harriet couldn't think why tonight was so important, couldn't think why Sue seemed so dedicated and withdrawn, and couldn't think either what to say or to do. Finally she said weakly: 'I'm sorry, Sue.'

'Nobody is exactly ecstatic.'

This enigmatic answer plunged Harriet into further difficulties. She reverted to her general, panic-stricken theories that she was no good with people, did not understand them, could not love. Finally, pulling herself together, something she was lamentably used to doing, she said: 'Sue, you'd better tell me about it. I mean, I don't know whether you love him, or – '

'It's nothing to do with love. If you live in a small village, you just can't strut about with a bellyful of other people's babies. People talk: they *know*. They just don't care for it at all. Anyway,' she added, 'just think of me with a dear little baby on my hands. My mother would go berserk. Think of my awful, pompous brothers. I couldn't say I'd adopted it. Anyway, Jean Christophe would have an awful time with his mother. His father's dead, and he's the only child. Madame Lupin expects him to make a suitable marriage. In fact, she's practically arranged it.'

By now they were climbing rapidly up round the hairpin bends of a small rocky mountain: there were fir or pine trees on the skyline, and already these had become black, while the bare places of rock on the right-hand side of the road were an ephemeral, tender pink – the younger trees or bushes a sunlit golden green. It was very beautiful, and Harriet said so.

'Yeah. You could have done some nice painting here. Can't you stay a couple of nights?'

'I must go back, honestly.' She did not mention that she had stopped painting a long time ago, and that any mention of it hurt – like mentioning a stillborn child to its mother. This was the kind of analogy of a tragi-sentimental nature that people only make when they have had one half of the experience: but the comparison had struck Harriet's mind with all the dramatic force that her frantically disappointed nature had needed. Ever since then, some part of her kept on muttering that nothing was worth trying to do; that most people were either neutral or fairly kind, that even the fruitless and dull situation with Tim was just about what she deserved.

'It's sure good to have you, honey pie.' Sue gave her a quick little pat on the knee.

'It's extremely kind of you to have asked me.' The language joke has stopped, then, she thought.

They had turned off the mountain road and were approaching what looked like an endless cavern of plane trees – an avenue planted each side of the road. Motor bikes roared to and fro; cats ran frantically across the road; it was dusk now, and people were sitting outside their houses.

'What *is* going to happen?' Harriet asked.

'What's going to happen if everything pans out, is that Jean is coming over as soon as it's dark, and Michèle is asleep (that's his boring wife), pick up what he needs from the *pharmacie* – his cousin runs that – and come up to the villa.'

'I thought you said that Jean wasn't married – only sort of engaged.'

'I don't mean Jean Christophe, I mean Jean Gautier. Although Jean Christophe will probably come too if Jean can think of a good reason for getting him out.'

'Is Jean Gautier the local doctor?'

'Jesus, no! He's the electrician. Good grief!' she added, as though the idea of a local doctor was too absurd to be contemplated. 'Jean isn't bad at it, though,' she finished. 'He's better at building, that's what he's saving for. But he does all the abortions round here. That's why we have to wait till it's dark. He always does them then, because it's more difficult for people to know where he's going. Here we go.' She suddenly swung them violently to the left, up what looked like a cart track. She put her headlights on, and they bumped and jolted round a series of corners until, without any warning at all, they ended in a pile of gravel. 'Damn! I thought they were starting the drive this afternoon: it's that sod Jules: he only works when he's short of *pastis* – I might have known it.'

'Shall I get out and push?'

'We can try: I'm not in a very pushing mood, though.'

They tried, but with absolutely no success: Sue had driven too fast and got too far into the pile. Finally, Sue took a torch from her bag; Harriet got her case from the boot, only to find that she was in what was very nearly pitch darkness.

'Sorry: the battery's dead, just follow me.'

This was Sue's voice some yards ahead in the darkness. Harriet stumbled over scratchy bushes, and small rocks; she had the kind of ankles admired by many, but no good for the dark, and she twisted one quite soon.

In the end, they reached the house. This had, of course, no light, and the shutters were closed. Sue opened the front door with a huge key slung round her neck.

'Come on in, hon,' she said with her best Southern accent, which wasn't very good.

While she was lighting the oil lamp, Harriet noticed that there were no mosquito screens, and indeed their low predatory drone was at once to be heard. But Susan was rich! She had always been rich – by Harriet's standards, even when neither of them had seemed to have to worry about dough, much. She slapped the side of her neck inefficiently, and at the same time, saw that Susan's kitchen was well up to American standards *vis-à-vis* chrome, formica, and gadgets. When Susan lit the second lamp, the room looked bright and sterile. There was nothing in the way of food to be seen.

'What we both need is a good, stiff drink. What'll you have?' Susan was rummaging about in the fridge and getting out ice. 'Whisky, brandy or gin?'

'Brandy – and soda if you have it, please.' At this moment she felt as though she had just met Susan, who just happened to look very like somebody she had once known.

'Sure – we have Perrier, lady. Nothing like it. I'll do the same.'

By the time they both had drinks in their hands, Harriet had been distinctly bitten four times and wondered whether there were *any* screens in the house.

'Could I go to the loo?'

'Sure. Hang on while I find me a torch that actually works. Here you are. The john's second right down there.' She opened another door in the kitchen and made a vague gesture.

Harriet walked cautiously down the tiled passage. Her ankle hurt, she was thirsty and tired, and suddenly remembered the wonderful showers at Mrs Mouncey's villa. The loo proved to have no screens either, so that was probably that. Remorse about Sue assailed her. Perhaps she had been desperately keeping up a front living in a small, obscure village because that was the cheapest thing to do. And now, to be facing what sounded like the most primitive butchery, having driven all the way to Marseille to collect her . . . there was no loo paper and no basin. She felt sticky, dispirited, and determined to make the brandy do her some good.

Susan had lit a Chesterfield and was looking at it distastefully. 'At least when this is over, I'll like smoking again,' she said as Harriet came in.

'Do you mind if I smoke?'

'Go ahead. And get on to your brandy. I want another.' Her small, freckled face looked momentarily frightened.

Harriet, when she had sipped her drink (goodness, it was strong!), said tentatively: 'Wouldn't it be better if you came back to England with me? I mean – mightn't it be safer? I could put you up: I've got a bed in my other room, and I could easily get the money – ' this last was not in the least true: but Harriet felt compelled to say it, in case poor Sue was really going through all this midnight fear and anxiety because she couldn't afford any other way.

'No: this'll be fine. Jean has done dozens of them. He's awfully careful.'

Harriet thought of her huge, newish looking Cadillac as Susan poured another large brandy and tried to top Harriet's drink up. She couldn't be really poor. She said that she really had better not drink any more before food, or she would be drunk. And useless, she added, although quite what her use might turn out to be was still a mystery to her. Susan looked rather blank.

'I'm not sure what we've got. Corn Flakes, anyway. And there may be a bit of *pâté*, but this morning I thought it'd gone off. There's some peppermint-creams some guy brought when he came to stay in the other house. Look in the fridge, and see what you can see.'

Harriet looked. The mosquitoes were now homing in on her as though she were London Airport. There was not much to see in the fridge, and what there was did not seem in any way inviting. There was a bit of *pâté*, dark and slippery and dangerous-looking. There was also a plate of very old crêpy-looking grapes, a withered lemon and some milk. Looking up rather desperately from this unfruitful hunt, she said: 'Do you, by any chance, have any anti-mosquito stuff?'

'Harry, I don't. I don't have a thing. I don't seem to be their meat, and I keep on trying to remember to put it on shopping lists and just don't seem to get around to it. Are you being bitten to death?'

'Yes,' said Harriet simply. The first ones were swelling up into their hard, itchy lumps that she knew she would scratch until she drew blood. She was hungry, tired, and baffled. 'Don't you eat in the evenings?' she asked with a touch of petulance.

'I don't bother. I'd take you down to the village, only we can't move the car, and I daren't miss Jean. Have some Corn Flakes; I don't think the milk is off.'

She prepared this simple meal for Harriet while drinking her third brandy, sat her down at the white formica table and pressed her to have more to drink. The milk *was* off, so Harriet accepted more brandy and lit a Gauloise.

'Have the grapes; they need eating up,' Susan said.

For a moment, Harriet hated her. It was a bit much to come all this way only to find a mosquito-ridden and cupboard-bare house. She thought of all the trouble she took when people came to her tiny flat. The dash to Soho in her lunch hour, to buy fresh sardines, interesting vegetables and cheeses. Tim always said that she took too much trouble, in *his* eyes, at least, but, she had soon discovered, any less than too much hardly amounted to trouble at all. If Sue really cared about her, wouldn't she at least have provided some food? No: the answer had always been, and was now, no. But an egg or some cheese would surely have been easy? 'I can't eat these grapes,' she announced: trying to show some spirit nearly always turned out to be rude.

'Listen! It's them: at least they've come.'

Harriet listened: over and above the ominous drone of mosquitoes, she heard what sounded like a very tiny car being abused at great speed. There was a small explosion on the gravel, doors slamming more times than four doors would slam, and feet outside – they could not tell how many. There were light taps with an intimate rhythm on the kitchen door: Sue had got to her feet, opened it immediately and let two men and one woman into the room.

'Voici Arlette,' the older man said briefly.

'Bonsoir, Arlette, je vous présente mon amie, Harriet. Elle part demain pour Londres. Voici Jean, et Jean Christophe.'

Harriet found herself shaking hands with all three of them; each one responded 'Madame'. Then they all sat round the table and Sue produced a bottle of wine and glasses. Harriet, too, was offered some wine: everybody excepting Arlette and Sue smoked.

There was a complete silence, which, though she felt it was intimate between the three French and Sue, simply mounted her own feeling of tension. She tried to deploy this by noticing the friends of her friend. Jean, the abortionist, was a heavy, dark man who looked as though no feat of strength could ever be beyond him. He wore a dark blue shirt with the sleeves rolled up to expose arms rounded with muscle and covered with dark hair. Beside him, Jean Christophe looked like some wild but faun-like creature. He too was dark, but very slender and wiry: he had the whitest teeth she had ever seen in her life and a capacity for stillness that made Harriet feel that, if she were alone with him, she would hear his heart beating. She felt comfortable about him. Arlette looked discontented and intelligent, excepting when either Sue or big Jean spoke to her, whereupon her face changed completely by her smile, both affectionate and sardonic.

'Heat water,' Jean told her briefly, and at once she fetched a saucepan, filled it nearly full of water, and lit the gas on one of the stove burners. 'Et un cendrier pour le fauve là.' Everybody laughed but Harriet, who saw Jean Christophe blush and shift his feet; he had been letting the ash accumulate at the end of his cigarette until about two inches of it had fallen to the tiled floor. Then everybody talked, and Harriet by listening as hard as she could gathered that big Jean was telling Sue that she was a stupid little cabbage driving her car into the middle of the heap of gravel. Sue replied defensively, mentioning several times the name of Jules, at which Arlette broke into a flood of sardonic reminiscence, which included an imitation of Jules that made everybody rock with laughter except for Jean Christophe, who gave a succession of fleeting smiles when he was not looking at the wine in his hands or at Harriet. The water boiled, and Jean took two things (instruments?) out of the small pack that hung round his back and dropped them in. 'Alors; vingt minutes,' he said. A moment of terror struck Sue's face, and Harriet saw her glance at Jean Christophe, but he was looking carefully at the end of his cigarette, as though it had nothing to do with him.

'If only I could speak French!' Harriet thought, realizing that this was what she had been thinking ever since the three of them arrived. The thought came to the surface because she realized that Sue was talking to big Jean about her. She got the point that Sue was explaining that she, Harriet, was one of her oldest friends, but after that she was lost. 'Marseille' was mentioned: something about her going on a train from there tomorrow and would big Jean be able to drive her, when suddenly Arlette exclaimed: 'Ah non!' There followed a torrent of conversation, until Harriet could bear it no longer, and touching Sue's arm said: 'Sue, *please,* tell me what this is all about.'

Sue lit a cigarette, took one puff and then stubbed it out before replying: 'Sorry, honey: it's just not being your night. Arlette says that if you want to get to England, you'll have to go tonight. There's a *grève* beginning tomorrow. A strike, railway shut-down except for freight. There *is* a train going out tonight, but nobody knows the time. Do you have to go tomorrow?'

'I have to: I have to be back at work.'

'Anyway, the strike could go on for a week or more. How about flying?'

'Can't do it.' Harriet did not want to explain that she simply hadn't the money for it.

Sue spoke rapidly to Arlette, who nodded, agreed and went out of the kitchen.

'She's going to try and telephone the station to find out the time. She may not get through, though.'

'But how can I *get* to Marseille? You certainly can't drive me.'

Sue turned to both the Jeans, impartially, as though they

155

were almost one person, and asked a brief question. The younger Jean answered monosyllabically, and Sue said: 'Jean will drive you.'

'It's very kind of him,' Harriet murmured, and as though he understood her perfectly, the younger Jean looked up at her suddenly with a smile both fleeting and mysterious, and said: 'C'est la moindre des choses, Mademoiselle.'

The larger Jean looked at his watch, and indicated that it was time. Sue leapt to her feet, but then stood transfixed there: Harriet got up from the table as well; she imagined that if there was any use she could be it must be now, and fear that she would in some way fail her friend assailed her. But Jean, carrying the pan, took Sue gently by the arm and led her out of the room. Harriet could hear them going upstairs together. She and the younger Jean were left alone. He offered her a cigarette, and while he was lighting it for her, she noticed that his hands, although the nails were broken and the skin hard, were a beautiful shape. His eyes avoided hers while he lit the cigarette, and while he was lighting his own, and afterwards he simply stared at the table. Harriet nearly thanked him, but then felt that this might lead to a conversation and she would be sunk, so she simply smiled at him. A clock ticked – like a metronome against the crowded sound of the cicadas. Arlette came back into the room. She jerked her head upwards as she asked Jean something and he nodded. She then burst into a voluble description of her telephone call, eventually turning to Harriet and clearly explaining to her about the train. 'Trois heures moins le quart,' she said several times, and Jean held up his three fingers and then cut the tip of his fourth finger with the other hand. 'Je comprends,' said Harriet. A quarter to three! And there would probably be no sleeping compartments left on the train, or they would be first class, or there simply wouldn't be any. Oh well. She offered Arlette and Jean more wine; both declined, but she helped herself. There was no other form of sustenance; she wanted badly to scratch her mosquito bites and hoped that the wine would help her to leave them alone.

Doing nothing in silence would make that impossible.

What seemed to Harriet a long time later, but was in fact only a few minutes, big Jean came down alone. 'Montez, Mademoiselle, s'il vous plaît,' he said slowly and carefully to Harriet, as he both looked at her and held the door open. Harriet got up, went through the door, to find herself immediately faced with a staircase behind it. Jean shut the door after her, whereupon she could hardly see at all, except a fortunate glimmer coming from a half-open door somewhere to the right at the top of the stairs. In her bedroom, Sue was lying on the bed on a blue towel. She wore simply her sleeveless shirt, and there was a pail beside the bed. Her face looked as though some faintly luminescent green light was shining upon it, and she was shivering.

'Could you get me another towel, honey?' she said in a voice diminished by either shock, fear or pain, Harriet was not sure. She fetched the towel from the adjacent bathroom, laid it over Sue and began to tuck it in.

'No, I can't have it tucked in. Any minute now, I'll have to shoot out and sit on that awful pail.'

'Can't you use the lavatory? I mean, wouldn't it be more comfortable?'

'It would, but Jean says he's got to see that everything's come out. He's got to wait, poor sod, until I've got rid of everything.'

'Poor Sue; I'm so sorry. Listen – apparently I've got to go tonight, as you know. But not for ages. The train leaves at three moins le quart.'

Sue smiled weakly. 'Well done, at least you're learning some French. I'm so sorry all that had to happen – Christ! Here it comes.' She was out of the bed in a single movement, and then sat on the pail. Harriet held out her hand, and Sue squeezed it.

'It's all right,' she said: 'It's on its way. It doesn't hurt.' Her face began to sweat. 'But it isn't exactly enjoyable.' Harriet knelt by her and went on holding her hand. There was what Harriet could only describe as a stench of hot blood. This nauseated her, but she knew that she must be oblivious of it. After all, nurses in hospitals ... She was glad she wasn't a nurse. She wasn't kind enough, or tough enough, or, indeed, anything enough. Then, suddenly it was better; Sue had become a small, vulnerable animal, entirely taken over by her body, and somehow impersonal and pathetic because of it. 'Not over yet. He said there might be a waiting time in between.' She panted like a small animal as well.

'I'm going to fetch a sponge for your face,' Harriet said, with the first air of authority she had experienced for years. Sue nodded, and then was taken over again. Harriet gently disentangled from Sue's cold and demanding clutch, and went to the bathroom. This time, as she ran a sponge under the hot tap, and surprisingly very hot water soon emerged from it, she noticed that the bathroom was also modern and immaculate – rather like the bathroom in a first-class hotel. That was to say that it had every gadget; gleaming tiles, a bidet, shower and bath and basin, but no sign that Sue used it at all, except for the sponge.

When she went back, Sue said, 'Getting on nicely'; her eyes were gleaming with tears. Harriet gently sponged her face, and fetched the towel to drape round her for warmth and dignity. 'Poor Sue: dear Sue,' she kept saying, and as though she could not understand the words, but only her tone of voice, Sue kept looking at her dumbly. After a while, of no duration that either of them could have measured, Sue said, 'It might be over now. Will you ask Jean to come up?'

'Of course.' Harriet left her, and went carefully down the stairs, felt for the latch of the door, but before she had found it, Jean was there. Harriet said: 'She wants you,' in English, but he understood, and went fast but heavily up the stairs.

Harriet, uncertain what she should do now, stood uneasily by the door to the kitchen. The etiquette of who could be where and when was obvious, she felt, to everybody except-ing herself. Arlette, without a word, handed her some brandy and a cigarette. Harriet, touched by the gestures, accepted both, neither of which she wanted. The other Jean looked significantly at the clock and at Harriet. 'Oh God! I'm going to have to go before it's all over.' This made her feel both treacherous and selfish. She nodded back, and went upstairs again.

When she entered the room, Sue was sitting on the pail. She said, 'It's not over. Jean says I must just stay here quietly.' She then said something to Jean, who passed his hand over her dank hair in a manner both kind and commanding. He then spoke to Sue, who said, 'Jean says that Jean will drive you to Marseille. You'll be all right with him. You ought to go now to get a seat. I'm so glad, honey. Don't worry about me.'

'I feel awful leaving you.'

'I feel awful having let you come.'

'Will you really be all right?'

'Natch. You can't possibly stay. If you're afraid of flying you'd be done for. The strike might go on for ages. Nobody knows. I'll call you. Oh!' She bent her head.

Harriet went uncertainly up to her and kissed the damp cold forehead from which the fringe had been sponged. 'I'm sorry,' she said again, and the inadequacy echoed inside her.

'Balls. Come again: I'm not like this all the time.' She looked at Harriet as though she passionately wanted her to confirm this.

'Of course you're not. Will you call me as soon as you feel like it? I'd like to know.'

'O.K. Be seeing you.' Sue shut her eyes, as though the parting was done. Harriet, with one glance at Jean, who nodded to her reassuringly, went down again.

In the kitchen, Jean the younger was waiting for her, her bag in his hand. Arlette shook her hand after Harriet had put on her jacket, and said: 'Au revoir, Mademoiselle.' Then, her eyes snapping with a kind of knowing cynicism, she said something very quickly to the younger Jean, who simply blushed and as usual looked at the floor. He took Harriet's hand, and led her out of the house into the darkness. This seemed not to trouble him at all, as he found the car as quickly and easily as though it had been broad daylight. It was some kind of van, the kind with two seats in front and a great deal of nebulous room behind. He opened Harriet's door for her with formality, and while he was putting her case in the back and getting into the driver's seat, Harriet had seconds to think about him. *He* had done this to Sue: but he seemed almost impervious: heartless and sexy, that was what he must be. She began to dislike and then to hate him, and to dread the drive, which she knew to be a long one, with somebody she could neither talk to nor like.

For the first few miles, Harriet simply felt a mounting tension of dislike, contempt, and rage, that he should have got her best friend Sue into such a situation so calmly. She began to wish that he understood English, so that she could tell him what she thought of him. But he couldn't, and so all her pent-up hatred was only exacerbated by silence. He did not speak: simply drove well and fast through the mostly dark countryside. After about twenty minutes, Harriet felt so awful about leaving her friend and being unable to attack or defend on her account that she found tears were slipping at a remarkable and silent speed down her face.

As though he instantly sensed this, Jean stopped the car. He stopped it in one of the innumerable places for people to break down or have picnics. When he switched off the engine, Harriet sobbed aloud: she had not expected him to stop, had no idea why he did so, and could not say anything effective to him about it. With the engine stopped the sound that she made seemed worse than ever. Jean turned to her and took her in his arms. She tried to strike him, and heard him laugh – a warm sound of certainty and understanding. He opened his door and took Harriet with him. Outside, she felt her knees giving way; her ankle still hurt, and she felt weak and paralysed. Jean picked her up in his arms and carried her a small distance from the car. He laid her on the ground, which seemed sandy and smelled of thyme, knelt by her, and began, very gently, stripping off her clothes. He did this in such a way that she did not seem to have thought about it. When he had taken all her clothes from her, he immediately began to caress her. No word was spoken, and in Harriet this achieved a kind of release. He was both sensitive to her and assured, and his hands running casually, tentatively down her body created a passive, over-still response that he thoroughly understood. He kissed her: her head, her ears, her mouth, her breasts, her thighs and her hands. She could not see, only feel him, and long before he stripped from his jeans, at last, she no longer cared what he was or had done, was incapable of thought, had only the need for the first time in her life. Tim had always said that women should be talked to, and she had accepted this, without any choice of what he talked about. Jean said nothing: he prepared her and took her, and the release, the radiant pleasure for Harriet, was like going to some new country as somebody else. He was extraordinarily careful, patient, intent, and waited for her until the end. When it was over, he encompassed her with his arms and began to caress her again as though they were at the beginning. Harriet turned to him and kissed him. In a way, it was the first kiss she had ever given in her life.

After a time, she had no idea how long, he took her again, and this was different; she had no fears, no uncertainty, was no longer passive and they were entirely together. Afterwards, he put his face against hers, and laughed; it was pleasure, satisfaction and joy. They were still together like that, until they could hear all the minuscule night creaks and mutters of the country were round them.

Then, a few minutes later, he began to dress her, with the same care and finesse that he had used when he had taken off her clothes. He also dressed himself, very quickly, took her hands and said: 'Est-ce que tu as faim?' She smiled in the dark, and he passed his hand over her face and knew.

They got back into the van again; again he put her in her seat formally, got into his, and drove off. He stopped at a very small café a few kilometres further on. 'Have we time?'

she said, realizing as she did so that she was ravenous but didn't care.

'We have time,' he answered.

The café had a small vine-covered terrace, but this was dark, and Jean pushed through the bead curtains. Inside, there was a small bar and four or five tables. Jean placed her at one of them and then went to talk to the *patron*. While he was ordering some food, she turned round in her chair to observe herself in the spotted mirror on the wall behind her. Her hair had fallen down: very small leaves and even twigs were entangled there, and her face had an expression that she had never seen before so that she looked at it for some seconds. 'I'm beautiful!' she thought. 'I have become beautiful': and then, because her nature was still both anxious and fearful, she wondered whether it would last. She tried to smooth back her hair with her hands, but had no desire to put it up. Jean came back with two glasses of *pastis*. He handed her one, and then sat opposite her. They both drank, and now Jean met her eyes frequently, and every time he did so, he smiled with a mixture of conspiracy and affection.

Unbelievably soon the food arrived. A plate of bread, oven-hot dishes with two eggs sizzling on each, and a board with three cheeses upon it, not one of which Harriet could recognize. They both ate ravenously; the *patron* was engaged upon what sounded like a political conversation with an old friend who seemed to agree with every word he said: no notice was taken of Harriet or Jean. When they had eaten, Jean said, 'Du café?' and Harriet felt herself colouring as she inclined her head and murmured, 'Merci.' 'Oui, ou non?' 'Oui.' While he went to get it, she wondered why saying thank you seemed a negation. The whole thing was mysterious and amazing: in one way she felt that she knew Jean better than she had ever known anyone – in another, not at all.

Scalding coffee in small, thick, white cups arrived. They smoked with this, and the moment it was over, Jean went and paid the bill and indicated that they should go – at once.

He said good night to the *patron*, and Harriet echoed this as he led her outside to the dark. He put her in the van once more, and drove even faster to Marseille. Harriet seemed to have no thoughts at all during the journey: only the consciousness of sitting beside him, of seeing sometimes his profile and his hands on the steering wheel in the headlights of occasional cars coming towards them; the spasmodic avenues of planes with their scarred trunks and dusty leaves in the headlights, the aromatic warmth of the air, the velvet bulk of some small hill, and then the country flattening, descending to the sea and the marigold lights of Marseille.

At the station, Jean parked, and got her case out of the van even before Harriet, in a dream still, had tried her door. He opened it for her. 'Vous avez un billet?'

'Non.'

'N'importe.' He led her to the ticket office which, even at this time of the night or morning, had a small queue.

'Couchette?' Harriet asked when her turn came.

'Ah non. Toutes les couchettes sont prises.' He gave her a look of indifference and exhaustion, and then looked at her again, and smiled faintly with admiring commiseration.

Jean found the right barrier and they began to walk up the train looking for a seat. This was difficult to find: people were crowded six a side, even on the wooden benches. At last Jean saw a possible place, if the other occupants would move up. This he not only got them to do, he secured a corner seat for Harriet. He put her case on top of many other people's things on the rack.

'Alors: au revoir, Mademoiselle,' he said; picked up her hand and kissed it with the formality of a bored nobleman. 'Oh *no*!' Harriet screamed silently inside. 'Not like that!' But it seemed to be so, and she leant out of the window, as he walked away. He did not look back. She remained at the window, until she felt that somehow or other she could face the other occupants: she *had* to; there was no choice at all. She edged her way back to the seat by the far window, and held her hands tightly over her mouth to stop herself, until her mouth felt bruised by her teeth.

And then, without the slightest warning, he was back. He beckoned to her, and again she stumbled past the other sleepy passengers, who were either cross or stertorous. He opened the carriage door. In his hands were a chocolate bar and a small bunch of violets. He put them into her hands, put his arms round her and kissed first her forehead and then her mouth. When he felt her tears, he kissed both her eyes, and said: 'Comment t'appelles-tu?'

'Harriet.'

'Arriette,' he repeated. 'Belle et tendre. Arriette. Bonne nuit.'

She nodded, clung to him a moment, and then he gently disengaged her and put her back into the carriage. This time he looked at her until she had once more found her place, raised his right hand in a valedictory salute and was gone.

Harriet sat, holding the chocolate bar and the violets: tears now streamed down her face, but she did not notice this, until an old woman dressed in black with thick black stockings and black gym shoes laid an overworked brown hand on her lap and said: 'Pauvre, pauvre petite.'

Harriet nodded and tried to smile, but the old woman had the courtesy to say no more and require nothing of her.

When the train began to move, Harriet found a small white handkerchief in her bag. She wiped her face and neck and then put the flowers (they smelled only like a memory of violets) into the handkerchief, which she carefully wrapped round their stalks. She looked at the bar of chocolate. These were his presents to her: she would never eat the chocolate, and the violets must never die. Sue crossed her mind once or twice before exhaustion overtook her: affectionate, distant, now impersonal thoughts. Tim also crossed her mind: she would go back to work when she could bear it, but she would never bear to see him again. She had no need; life was neither so poor nor so thin a business as she had thought.

By the time the train reached Paris, many hours later, she

was wearily awake: too tired to try to go on sleeping in the same position, realizing that what she had always known as life was inexorably drawing nearer. She wanted to wash. She staggered along the corridor to the overworked *toilettes* and washed her face and hands. There was nothing bearable to dry them on. There was no breakfast on that train, or the one she had to change into. She eventually ate the chocolate bar very slowly – remembering his face when he had given it to her.

By the time she reached Victoria Station, the violets were crushed and limply dead. But when she finally reached her small, familiar, but now alien flat, and fell upon her bed without attempting to unpack or even to undress, there were still pieces of thyme in her hair.

THREE MILES UP

THERE was absolutely nothing like it.

An unoriginal conclusion, and one that he had drawn a hundred times during the last fortnight. Clifford would make some subtle and intelligent comparison, but he, John, could only continue to repeat that it was quite unlike anything else. It had been Clifford's idea, which, considering Clifford, was surprising. When you looked at him, you would not suppose him capable of it. However, John reflected, he had been ill, some sort of breakdown these clever people went in for, and that might account for his uncharacteristic idea of hiring a boat and travelling on canals. On the whole, John had to admit, it was a good idea. He had never been on a canal in his life, although he had been in almost every kind of boat, and thought he knew a good deal about them; so much, indeed, that he had embarked on the venture in a light-hearted, almost a patronizing manner. But it was not nearly as simple as he had imagined. Clifford, of course, knew nothing about boats; but he had admitted that almost everything had gone wrong with a kind of devilish versatility which had almost frightened him. However, that was all over, and John, who had learned painfully all about the boat and her engine, felt that the former at least had run her gamut of disaster. They had run out of food, out of petrol, and out of water; had dropped their windlass into the deepest lock, and, more humiliating, their boathook into the side-pond. The head had come off the hammer. They had been disturbed for one whole night by a curious rustling in the cabin, like a rat in a paper bag, when there was no paper, and, so far as they knew, no rat. The battery had failed and had had to be recharged. Clifford had put his elbow through an already cracked window in the cabin. A large piece of

rope had wound itself round the propeller with a malignant
intensity which required three men and half a morning to
unravel. And so on, until now there was really nothing left to
go wrong, unless one of them drowned, and surely it was
impossible to drown in a canal.

'I suppose one might easily drown in a lock?' he asked
aloud.

'We must be careful not to fall into one,' Clifford replied.

'What?' John steered with fierce concentration, and never
heard anything people said to him for the first time, almost
on principle.

'I said we must be careful not to fall *into* a lock.'

'Oh. Well there aren't any more now until after the Junction. Anyway, we haven't yet, so there's really no reason why
we should start now. I only wanted to know whether we'd
drown if we did.'

'Sharon might.'

'What?'

'Sharon might.'

'Better warn her then. She seems agile enough.' His concentrated frown returned, and he settled down again to the
wheel. John didn't mind where they went, or what happened, so long as he handled the boat, and all things considered, he handled her remarkably well. Clifford planned
and John steered: and until two days ago they had both
quarrelled and argued over a smoking and unusually tem-
peramental primus. Which reminded Clifford of Sharon.
Her advent and the weather were really their two un-
adulterated strokes of good fortune. There had been no rain,
and Sharon had, as it were, dropped from the blue on to the
boat, where she speedily restored domestic order, stimulated
evening conversation, and touched the whole venture with
her attractive being: the requisite number of miles each day
were achieved, the boat behaved herself, and admirable
meals were steadily and regularly prepared. She had, in fact,
identified herself with the journey, without making the
slightest effort to control it: a talent which many women

were supposed in theory to possess, when, in fact, Clifford reflected gloomily, most of them were bored with the whole thing, or tried to dominate it.

Her advent was a remarkable, almost a miraculous, piece of luck. He had, after a particularly ill-fed day, and their failure to dine at a small hotel, desperately telephoned all the women he knew who seemed in the least suitable (and they were surprisingly few), with no success. They had spent a miserable evening, John determined to argue about everything, and he, Clifford, refusing to speak; until, both in a fine state of emotional tension, they had turned in for the night. While John snored, Clifford had lain distraught, his resentment and despair circling round John and then touching his own smallest and most random thoughts; until his mind found no refuge and he was left, divided from it, hostile and afraid, watching it in terror racing on in the dark like some malignant machine utterly out of his control.

The next day things had proved no better between them, and they had continued throughout the morning in a silence which was only occasionally and elaborately broken. They had tied up for lunch beside a wood, which hung heavy and magnificent over the canal. There was a small clearing beside which John then proposed to moor, but Clifford failed to achieve the considerable leap necessary to stop the boat; and they had drifted helplessly past it. John flung him a line, but it was not until the boat was secured, and they were safely in the cabin, that the storm had broken. John, in attempting to light the primus, spilt a quantity of paraffin on Clifford's bunk. Instantly all his despair of the previous evening had contracted. He hated John so much that he could have murdered him. They both lost their tempers, and for the ensuing hour and a half had conducted a blazing quarrel which, even at the time, secretly horrified them both in its intensity.

It had finally ended with John striding out of the cabin, there being no more to say. He had returned almost at once, however.

'I say, Clifford. Come and look at this.'

'At what?'

'Outside, on the bank.'

For some unknown reason Clifford did get up and did look. Lying face downwards quite still on the ground, with her arms clasping the trunk of a large tree, was a girl.

'How long has she been there?'

'She's asleep.'

'She can't have been asleep all the time. She must have heard some of what we said.'

'Anyway, who is she? What is she doing here?'

Clifford looked at her again. She was wearing a dark twill shirt and dark trousers, and her hair hung over her face, so that it was almost invisible. 'I don't know. I suppose she's alive?'

John jumped cautiously ashore. 'Yes, she's alive all right. Funny way to lie.'

'Well, it's none of our business anyway. Anyone can lie on a bank if they want to.'

'Yes, but she must have come in the middle of our row, and it does seem queer to stay, and then go to sleep.'

'Extraordinary,' said Clifford wearily. Nothing was really extraordinary, he felt, nothing. 'Are we moving on?'

'Let's eat first. I'll do it.'

'Oh, I'll do it.'

The girl stirred, unclasped her arms, and sat up. They had all stared at each other for a moment, the girl slowly pushing the hair from her forehead. Then she had said: 'If you will give me a meal, I'll cook it.'

Afterwards they had left her to wash up, and had walked about the wood, while Clifford suggested to John that they ask the girl to join them. 'I'm sure she'd come,' he said. 'She didn't seem at all clear about what she was doing.'

'We can't just pick somebody up out of a wood,' said John, scandalized.

'Where do you suggest we pick them up? If we don't have someone, this holiday will be a failure.'

'We don't know anything about her.'

'I can't see that that matters very much. She seems to cook well. We can at least ask her.'

'All right. Ask her then. She won't come.'

When they returned to the boat, she had finished the washing-up, and was sitting on the floor of the cockpit, with her arms stretched behind her head. Clifford asked her; and she accepted as though she had known them a long time and they were simply inviting her to tea.

'Well, but look here,' said John, thoroughly taken aback. 'What about your things?'

'My things?' she looked inquiringly and a little defensively from one to the other.

'Clothes and so on. Or haven't you got any? Are you a gipsy or something? Where do you come from?'

'I am not a gipsy,' she began patiently; when Clifford, thoroughly embarrassed and ashamed, interrupted her.

'Really, it's none of our business who you are, and there is absolutely no need for us to ask you anything. I'm very glad you will come with us, although I feel we should warn you that we are new to this life, and anything might happen.'

'No need to warn me,' she said, and smiled gratefully at him.

After that, they both felt bound to ask her nothing; John because he was afraid of being made to look foolish by Clifford, and Clifford because he had stopped John.

'Good Lord, we shall never get rid of her; and she'll fuss about condensation,' John had muttered aggressively as he started the engine. But she was very young, and did not fuss about anything. She had told them her name, and settled down, immediately and easily: gentle, assured and unselfconscious to a degree remarkable in one so young. They were never sure how much she had overheard them, for she gave no sign of having heard anything. A friendly but uncommunicative creature.

The map on the engine box started to flap, and immediately John asked, 'Where are we?'

'I haven't been watching, I'm afraid. Wait a minute.'

'We just passed under a railway bridge,' John said helpfully.

'Right. Yes. About four miles from the Junction, I think. What's the time?'

'Five-thirty.'

'Which way are we going when we get to the Junction?'

'We haven't time for the big loop. I must be back in London by the fifteenth.'

'The alternative is to go up as far as the basin, and then simply turn round and come back, and who wants to do that?'

'Well, we'll know the route then. It'll be much easier coming back.'

Clifford did not reply. He was not attracted by the route being easier, and he wanted to complete his original plan.

'Let us wait till we get there.' Sharon appeared with tea and marmalade sandwiches.

'All right, let's wait.' Clifford was relieved.

'It'll be almost dark by five-thirty. I think we ought to have a plan,' John said. 'Thank you, Sharon.'

'Have tea first.' She curled herself on to the floor with her back to the cabin doors and a mug in her hands.

They were passing rows of little houses with gardens that backed on to the canal. They were long narrow strips, streaked with cinder paths, and crowded with vegetables and chicken-huts, fruit trees and perambulators; sometimes ending with fat white ducks, and sometimes in a tiny patch of grass with a bench on it.

'Would you rather keep ducks or sit on a bench?' asked Clifford.

'Keep ducks,' said John promptly. 'More useful. Sharon wouldn't mind which she did. Would you, Sharon?' He liked saying her name, Clifford noticed. 'You could be happy anywhere, couldn't you?' He seemed to be presenting her with the widest possible choice.

'I might *be* anywhere,' she answered after a moment's thought.

'Well you happen to be on a canal, and very nice for us.'

'In a wood, and then on a canal,' she replied contentedly, bending her smooth dark head over her mug.

'Going to be fine tomorrow,' said John. He was always a little embarrassed at any mention of how they found her and his subsequent rudeness.

'Yes. I like it when the whole sky is so red and burning and it begins to be cold.'

'*Are* you cold?' said John, wanting to worry about it: but she tucked her dark shirt into her troubles and answered composedly:

'Oh no. I am never cold.'

They drank their tea in a comfortable silence. Clifford started to read his map, and then said they were almost on to another sheet. 'New country,' he said with satisfaction. 'I've never been here before.'

'You make it sound like an exploration; doesn't he, Sharon?' said John.

'Is that a bad thing?' She collected the mugs. 'I am going to put these away. You will call me if I am wanted for anything.' And she went into the cabin again.

There was a second's pause, a minute tribute to her departure; and, lighting cigarettes, they settled down to stare at the long silent stretch of water ahead.

John thought about Sharon. He thought rather desperately that really they still knew nothing about her, and that when they went back to London they would in all probability never see her again. Perhaps Clifford would fall in love with her, and she would naturally reciprocate, because she was so young and Clifford was reputed to be so fascinating and intelligent, and because women were always foolish and loved the wrong man. He thought all these things with equal intensity, glanced cautiously at Clifford, and supposed he was thinking about her; then wondered what she would be like in London, clad in anything else but her dark trousers and shirt. The engine coughed; and he turned to it in relief.

Clifford was making frantic calculations of time and distance; stretching their time, and diminishing the distance, and groaning that with the utmost optimism they could not be made to fit. He was interrupted by John swearing at the engine, and then for no particular reason he remembered Sharon, and reflected with pleasure how easily she left the mind when she was not present, how she neither obsessed nor possessed one in her absence, but was charming to see.

The sun had almost set when they reached the Junction, and John slowed down to neutral while they made up their minds. To the left was the straight cut which involved the longer journey originally planned; and curving away to the right was the short arm which John advocated. The canal was fringed with rushes, and there was one small cottage with no light in it. Clifford went into the cabin to tell Sharon where they were, and then, as they drifted slowly in the middle of the Junction, John suddenly shouted: 'Clifford! What's the third turning?'

'There are only two.' Clifford reappeared. 'Sharon is busy with dinner.'

'No, look. Surely that is another cut.'

Clifford stared ahead. 'Can't see it.'

'Just to the right of the cottage. Look. It's not so dark as all that.'

Then Clifford saw it very plainly. It seemed to wind away from the cottage on a fairly steep curve, and the rushes shrouding it from anything but the closest view were taller than the rest.

'Have another look at the map. I'll reverse for a bit.'

'Found it. It's just another arm. Probably been abandoned,' said Clifford eventually.

The boat had swung round; and now they could see the continuance of the curve dully gleaming ahead, and banked by reeds.

'Well, what shall we do?'

'Getting dark. Let's go up a little way, and moor. Nice quiet mooring.'

'With some nice quiet mudbanks,' said John grimly. 'Nobody uses that.'

'How do you know?'

'Well look at it. All those rushes, and it's sure to be thick with weed.'

'Don't go up it then. But we shall go aground if we drift about like this.'

'*I* don't mind going up it,' said John doggedly. 'What about Sharon?'

'What about her?'

'Tell her about it.'

'We've found a third turning,' Clifford called above the noise of the primus through the cabin door.

'One you had not expected?'

'Yes. It looks very wild. We were thinking of going up it.'

'Didn't you say you wanted to explore?' she smiled at him.

'You are quite ready to try it? I warn you we shall probably run hard aground. Look out for bumps with the primus.'

'I am quite ready, and I am quite sure we shan't run aground,' she answered with charming confidence in their skill.

They moved slowly forward in the dusk. Why they didn't run aground, Clifford could not imagine: John really was damned good at it. The canal wound and wound, and the reeds grew not only thick on each bank, but in clumps across the canal. The light drained out of the sky into the water and slowly drowned there; the trees and the banks became heavy and black.

Clifford began to clear things away from the heavy dew which had begun to rise. After two journeys he remained in the cabin, while John crawled on, alone. Once, on a bend, John thought he saw a range of hills ahead with lights on them, but when he was round the curve and had time to look again he could see no hills: only a dark indeterminate waste of country stretched ahead.

He was beginning to consider the necessity of mooring, when they came to a bridge; and shortly after he saw a dark mass which he took to be houses. When the boat had crawled for another fifty yards or so, he stopped the engine, and drifted in absolute silence to the bank. The houses, about half a dozen of them, were much nearer than he had at first imagined, but there were no lights to be seen. Distance is always deceptive in the dark, he thought, and jumped ashore with a bow line. When, a few minutes later, he took a sounding with the boathook, the water proved unexpectedly deep; and he concluded that by incredible good fortune they had moored at the village wharf. He made everything fast, and joined the others in the cabin with mixed feelings of pride and resentment; that he should have achieved so much under such difficult conditions, and that they (by 'they' he meant Clifford) should have contributed so little towards the achievement. He found Clifford reading *Bradshaw's Guide to the Canals and Navigable Rivers* in one corner and Sharon, with her hair pushed back behind her ears, bending over the primus with a knife. Her ears are pale, exactly the colour of her face, he thought; wanted to touch them; then felt horribly ashamed, and hated Clifford.

'Let's have a look at Bradshaw,' he said, as though he had not noticed Clifford reading it.

But Clifford handed him the book in the most friendly manner, remarking that he couldn't see where they were. 'In fact you have surpassed yourself with your brilliant navigation. We seem to be miles from anywhere.'

'What about your famous ordnance?'

'It's not on any sheet I have. The new one I thought we should use only covers the loop we planned. There is precisely three-quarters of a mile of this canal shown on the present sheet and then we run off the map. I suppose there must once have been trade here, but I cannot imagine what, or where.'

'I expect things change,' said Sharon. 'Here is the meal.'

'How can you see to cook?' asked John, eyeing his plate ravenously.

'There is a candle.'

'Yes, but we've selfishly appropriated that.'

'Should I need more light?' she asked, and looked troubled.

'There's no should about it. I just don't know how you do it, that's all. Chips exactly the right colour, and you never drop anything. It's marvellous.'

She smiled a little uncertainly at him and lit another candle. 'Luck, probably,' she said, and set it on the table.

They ate their meal, and John told them about the mooring. 'Some sort of village. I think we're moored at the wharf. I couldn't find any rings without the torch, so I've used the anchor.' This small shaft was intended for Clifford, who had dropped the spare torch-battery in the washing-up bowl, and forgotten to buy another. But it was only a small shaft, and immediately afterwards John felt much better. His aggression slowly left him, and he felt nothing but a peaceful and well-fed affection for the other two.

'Extraordinarily cut off this is,' he remarked over coffee.

'It's very pleasant in here. Warm, and extremely full of us.'

'Yes. I know. A quiet village, though, you must admit.'

'I shall believe in your village when I see it.'

'Then you would believe it?'

'No he wouldn't, Sharon. Not if he didn't want to, and couldn't find it on the map. That map!'

The conversation turned again to their remoteness, and to how cut off one liked to be and at what point it ceased to be desirable; to boats, telephones, and, finally, canals: which, Clifford maintained, possessed the perfect proportions of urbanity and solitude.

Hours later, when they had turned in for the night, Clifford reviewed the conversation, together with others they had had, and remembered with surprise how little Sharon had actually said. She listened to everything and occasionally, when they appealed to her, made some small composed remark which was oddly at variance with their passionate interest. 'She has an elusive quality of freshness about her,' he thought, 'which is neither naive nor stupid nor dull, and she invokes no responsibility. She does not want us to know what she was, or why we found her as we did, and curiously, I, at least, do not want to know. She is what women ought to be,' he concluded with sudden pleasure; and slept.

He woke the next morning to find it very late, and stretched out his hand to wake John.

'We've all overslept. Look at the time.'

'Good Lord! Better wake Sharon.'

Sharon lay between them on the floor, which they had ceded her because, oddly enough, it was the widest and most comfortable bed. She seemed profoundly asleep, but at the mention of her name sat up immediately, and rose, almost as though she had not been asleep at all.

The morning routine, which, involving the clothing of three people and shaving of two of them, was necessarily a long and complicated business, began. Sharon boiled water, and Clifford, grumbling gently, hoisted himself out of his bunk and repaired with a steaming jug to the cockpit. He put the jug on a seat, lifted the canvas awning, and leaned out. It was absolutely grey and still; a little white mist hung over the canal, and the country stretched out desolate and unkempt on every side with no sign of a living creature. The village, he thought; suddenly: John's village: and was possessed of a perilous uncertainty and fear. I am getting worse, he thought, this holiday is doing me no good. I am mad. I imagined that he said we moored by a village wharf. For several seconds he stood gripping the gunwale, and searching desperately for anything, huts, a clump of trees, which could in the darkness have been mistaken for a village. But there was nothing near the boat except tall rank rushes which did not move at all. Then, when his suspense was becoming unbearable, John joined him with another steaming jug of water.

'We shan't get anywhere at this rate,' he began; and then . . . 'Hullo! Where's my village?'

'I was wondering that,' said Clifford. He could almost have wept with relief, and quickly began to shave, deeply ashamed of his private panic.

'Can't understand it,' John was saying. It was no joke, Clifford decided, as he listened to his hearty puzzled ruminations.

At breakfast John continued to speculate upon what he had or had not seen, and Sharon listened intently while she filled the coffee-pot and cut bread. Once or twice she met Clifford's eye with a glance of discreet amusement.

'I must be mad, or else the whole place is haunted,' finished John comfortably. These two possibilities seemed to relieve him of any further anxiety in the matter, as he ate a huge breakfast and set about greasing the engine.

'Well,' said Clifford, when he was alone with Sharon. 'What do you make of that?'

'It is easy to be deceived in such matters,' she answered perfunctorily.

'Evidently. Still, John is an unlikely candidate, you must admit. Here, I'll help you dry.'

'Oh no. It is what I am here for.'

'Not entirely, I hope.'

'Not entirely.' She smiled and relinquished the cloth.

John eventually announced that they were ready to start. Clifford, who had assumed that they were to retrace their journey, was surprised, and a little alarmed, to find John intent upon continuing it. He seemed undeterred by the state of the canal, which, as Clifford immediately pointed out, rendered navigation both arduous and unrewarding. He announced that the harder it was, the more he liked it, adding very firmly, 'Anyway we must see what happens.'

'We shan't have time to do anything else.'

'Thought you wanted to explore.'

'I do, but . . . What do you think, Sharon?'

'I think John will have to be a very good navigator to

manage that.' She indicated the rush- and weed-ridden reach before them. 'Do you think it's possible?'

'Of course it's possible. I'll probably need some help though.'

'I'll help you,' she said.

So on they went.

They made incredibly slow progress. John enjoys showing off his powers to her, thought Clifford, half amused, half exasperated, as he struggled for the fourth time in an hour to scrape weeds off the propeller.

Sharon eventually retired to cook lunch.

'Surprising amount of water here,' John said suddenly.

'Oh?'

'Well, I mean, with all this weed and stuff, you'd expect the canal to have silted up. I'm sure nobody uses it.'

'The whole thing is extraordinary.'

'Is it too late in the year for birds?' asked Clifford later.

'No, I don't think so. Why?'

'I haven't heard one, have you?'

'Haven't noticed, I'm afraid. There's someone anyway. First sign of life.'

An old man stood near the bank watching them. He was dressed in corduroy and wore a straw hat.

'Good morning,' shouted John, as they drew nearer.

He made no reply, but inclined his head slightly. He seemed very old. He was leaning on a scythe, and as they drew almost level with him, he turned away and began slowly cutting rushes. A pile of them lay neatly stacked beside him.

'Where does this canal go? Is there a village further on?' Clifford and John asked simultaneously. He seemed not to hear, and as they chugged steadily past, Clifford was about to suggest that they stop and ask again, when he called after them: 'Three miles up you'll find the village. Three miles up that is,' and turned away to his rushes again.

'Well now we know something, anyway,' said John.

'We don't even know what the village is called.'

'Soon find out. Only three miles.'

'Three miles!' said Clifford darkly. 'That might mean anything.'

'Do you want to turn back?'

'Oh no, not now. I want to see this village now. My curiosity is thoroughly aroused.'

'Shouldn't think there'll be anything to see. Never been in such a wild spot. Look at it.'

Clifford looked at it. Half wilderness, half marsh, dank and grey and still, with single trees bare of their leaves; clumps of hawthorn that might once have been hedge, sparse and sharp with berries; and, in the distance, hills and an occasional wood: these were all one could see, beyond the lines of rushes which edged the canal winding ahead.

They stopped for a lengthy meal, which Sharon described as lunch and tea together, it being so late; and then, appalled at how little daylight was left, continued.

'We've hardly been any distance at all,' said John forlornly. 'Good thing there were no locks. I shouldn't think they'd have worked if there were.'

'*Much* more than three miles,' he said, about two hours later. Darkness was descending and it was becoming very cold.

'Better stop,' said Clifford.

'Not yet. I'm determined to reach that village.'

'Dinner is ready,' said Sharon sadly. 'It will be cold.'

'Let's stop.'

'You have your meal. I'll call if I want you.'

Sharon looked at them, and Clifford shrugged his shoulders. 'Come on. I will. I'm tired of this.'

They shut the cabin doors. John could hear the pleasant clatter of their meal, and just as he was coming to the end of the decent interval which he felt must elapse before he gave in, they passed under a bridge, the first of the day, and, clutching at any straw, he immediately assumed that it prefaced the village. 'I think we're nearly there,' he called.

Clifford opened the door. 'The village?'

'No, a bridge. Can't be far now.'

'You're mad, John. It's pitch dark.'

'You can see the bridge though.'

'Yes. Why not moor under it?'

'Too late. Can't turn round in this light, and she's not good at reversing. Must be nearly there. You go back, I don't need you.'

Clifford shut the door again. He was beginning to feel irritated with John behaving in this childish manner and showing off to impress Sharon. It was amusing in the morning, but really he was carrying it a bit far. Let him manage the thing himself then. When, a few minutes later, John shouted that they had reached the sought-after village, Clifford merely pulled back the little curtain over a cabin window, rubbed the condensation, and remarked that he could see nothing. 'No light at least.'

'He is happy anyhow,' said Sharon peaceably.

'Going to have a look around,' said John, slamming the cabin doors and blowing his nose.

'Surely you'll eat first?'

'If you've left anything. My God it's cold! It's *unnaturally* cold.'

'We won't be held responsible if he dies of exposure, will we?' said Clifford.

She looked at him, hesitated a moment, but did not reply, and placed a steaming plate in front of John. She doesn't want us to quarrel, Clifford thought, and with an effort of friendliness he asked: 'What does tonight's village look like?'

'Much the same. Only one or two houses, you know. But the old man called it a village.' He seemed uncommunicative; Clifford thought he was sulking. But after eating the meal, he suddenly announced, almost apologetically, 'I don't think I shall walk round. I'm absolutely worn out. You go if you like. I shall start turning in.'

'All right. I'll have a look. You've had a hard day.'

Clifford pulled on a coat and went outside. It was, as John said, incredibly cold and almost overwhelmingly silent. The clouds hung very low over the boat, and mist was rising everywhere from the ground, but he could dimly discern the black huddle of cottages lying on a little slope above the bank against which the boat was moored. He did actually set foot on shore, but his shoe sank immediately into a marshy hole. He withdrew it, and changed his mind. The prospect of groping round those dark and silent houses became suddenly distasteful, and he joined the others with the excuse that it was too cold and that he also was tired.

A little later, he lay half-conscious in a kind of restless trance, with John sleeping heavily opposite him. His mind seemed full of foreboding, fear of something unknown and intangible: he thought of them lying in warmth on the cold secret canal with desolate miles of water behind and probably beyond; the old man and the silent houses; John, cut off and asleep, and Sharon, who lay on the floor beside him. Immediately he was filled with a sudden and most violent desire for her, even to touch her, for her to know that he was awake.

'Sharon,' he whispered; 'Sharon, Sharon,' and stretched down his fingers to her in the dark.

Instantly her hand was in his, each smooth and separate finger warmly clasped. She did not move or speak, but his relief was indescribable and for a long while he lay in an ecstasy of delight and peace, until his mind slipped imperceptibly with her fingers into oblivion.

When he woke he found John absent and Sharon standing over the primus. 'He's outside,' she said.

'Have I overslept again?'

'It is late. I am boiling water for you now.'

'We'd better try and get some supplies this morning.'

'There is no village,' she said, in a matter-of-fact tone.

'What?'

'John says not. But we have enough food, if you don't mind this queer milk from a tin.'

'No, I don't mind,' he replied, watching her affectionately. 'It doesn't really surprise me,' he added after a moment.

'The village?'

'No village. Yesterday I should have minded awfully. Is that you, do you think?'

'Perhaps.'

'It doesn't surprise you about the village at all, does it? Do you love me?'

She glanced at him quickly, a little shocked, and said quietly: 'Don't you know?' then added: 'It doesn't surprise me.'

John seemed very disturbed. 'I don't like it,' he kept saying as they shaved. 'Can't understand it at all. I could have sworn there were houses last night. You saw them, didn't you?'

'Yes.'

'Well, don't you think it's very odd?'

'I do.'

'Everything looks the same as yesterday morning. I don't like it.'

'It's an adventure, you must admit.'

'Yes, but I've had enough of it. I suggest we turn back.'

Sharon suddenly appeared, and, seeing her, Clifford knew that he did not want to go back. He remembered her saying: 'Didn't you say you wanted to explore?' She would think him weak-hearted if they turned back all those dreary miles with nothing to show for it. At breakfast, he exerted himself in persuading John to the same opinion. John finally agreed to one more day, but, in turn, extracted a promise that they would then go back whatever happened. Clifford agreed to this, and Sharon for some inexplicable reason laughed at them both. So that eventually they prepared to set off in an atmosphere of general good humour.

Sharon began to fill the water-tank with their four-gallon can. It seemed too heavy for her, and John dropped the starter and leapt to her assistance.

She let him take the can and held the funnel for him. Together they watched the rich, even stream of water disappear.

'You shouldn't try to do that,' he said. 'You'll hurt your-self.'

'Gipsies do it,' she said.

'I'm awfully sorry about that. You know I am.'

'I shouldn't have minded if you had thought I was a gipsy.'

'I do like you,' he said, not looking at her. 'I do like you. You won't disappear altogether when this is over, will you?'

'You probably won't find I'll disappear for good,' she replied comfortingly.

'Come on,' shouted Clifford.

It's all right for *him* to talk to her, John thought, as he struggled to swing the starter. He just doesn't like me doing it; and he wished, as he had often begun to do, that Clifford was not there.

They had spasmodic engine trouble in the morning, which slowed them down; and the consequent halts, with the difficulty they experienced of mooring anywhere (the banks seemed nothing but marsh), were depressing and cold. Their good spirits evaporated: by lunch-time John was plainly irritable and frightened, and Clifford had begun to hate the grey silent land on either side, with the woods and hills which remained so consistently distant. They both wanted to give it up by then, but John felt bound to stick to his promise, and Clifford was secretly sure that Sharon wished to continue.

While she was preparing another late lunch, they saw a small boy who stood on what once had been the towpath watching them. He was bare-headed, wore corduroy, and had no shoes. He held a long reed, the end of which he chewed as he stared at them.

'Ask him where we are,' said John; and Clifford asked.

He took the reed out of his mouth, but did not reply.

'Where do you live then?' asked Clifford as they drew almost level with him.

'I told you. Three miles up,' he said; and then he gave a sudden little shriek of fear, dropped the reed, and turned to run down the bank the way they had come. Once he looked back, stumbled and fell, picked himself up sobbing, and ran faster. Sharon had appeared with lunch a moment before, and together they listened to his gasping cries growing fainter and fainter, until he had run himself out of their sight.

'What on earth frightened him?' said Clifford.

'I don't know. Unless it was Sharon popping out of the cabin like that.'

'Nonsense. But he was a very frightened little boy. And, I say, do you realize ...'

'He was a very foolish little boy,' Sharon interrupted. She was angry, Clifford noticed with surprise, really angry, white and trembling, and with a curious expression which he did not like.

'We might have got something out of him,' said John sadly.

'Too late now,' Sharon said. She had quite recovered herself.

They saw no one else. They journeyed on throughout the afternoon; it grew colder, and at the same time more and more airless and still. When the light began to fail, Sharon disappeared as usual to the cabin. The canal became more tortuous, and John asked Clifford to help him with the turns. Clifford complied unwillingly: he did not want to leave Sharon, but as it had been he who had insisted on their continuing, he could hardly refuse. The turns were nerve-racking, as the canal was very narrow and the light grew worse and worse.

'All right if we stop soon?' asked John eventually.

'Stop now if you like.'

'Well, we'll try and find a tree to tie up to. This swamp is awful. Can't think how that child ran.'

'That child ...' began Clifford anxiously; but John, who had been equally unnerved by the incident, and did not want to think about it, interrupted. 'Is there a tree ahead anywhere?'

'Can't see one. There's a hell of a bend coming though. Almost back on itself. Better slow a bit more.'

'Can't. We're right down as it is.'

They crawled round, clinging to the outside bank, which seemed always to approach them, its rushes to rub against their bows, although the wheel was hard over. John grunted with relief, and they both stared ahead for the next turn.

They were presented with the most terrible spectacle. The canal immediately broadened, until no longer a canal but a sheet, an infinity, of water stretched ahead; oily, silent, and still, as far as the eye could see, with no country edging it, nothing but water to the low grey sky above it. John had almost immediately cut out the engine, and now he tried desperately to start it again, in order to turn round. Clifford instinctively glanced behind them. He saw no canal at all, no inlet, but grasping and close to the stern of the boat, the reeds and rushes of a marshy waste closing in behind them. He stumbled to the cabin doors and pulled them open. It was very neat and tidy in there, but empty. Only one stern door of the cabin was free of its catch, and it flapped irregularly backwards and forwards with their movements in the boat.

There was no sign of Sharon at all.

MORE ABOUT PENGUINS, PELICANS
AND PUFFINS

For further information about books available from Penguins please write to Dept EP, Penguin Books Ltd, Harmondsworth, Middlesex UB7 ODA.

In the U.S.A.: For a complete list of books available from Penguins in the United States write to Dept DG, Penguin Books, 299 Murray Hill Parkway, East Rutherford, New Jersey 07073.

In Canada: For a complete list of books available from Penguins in Canada write to Penguin Books Canada Ltd, 2801 John Street, Markham, Ontario L3R 1B4.

In Australia: For a complete list of books available from Penguins in Australia write to the Marketing Department, Penguin Books Australia Ltd, P.O. Box 257, Ringwood, Victoria 3134.

In New Zealand: For a complete list of books available from Penguins in New Zealand write to the Marketing Department, Penguin Books (N.Z.) Ltd, P.O. Box 4019, Auckland 10.

In India: For a complete list of books available from Penguins in India write to Penguin Overseas Ltd, 706 Eros Apartments, 56 Nehru Place, New Delhi 110019.

FALLING IN PLACE
Ann Beattie

It's a hot, sullen summer on America's East Coast. As John and Louise Knapp bicker at their weekend marriage; as twelve-year-old Parker makes another trip to the shrink in New York; as Cynthia the English teacher clings to her freaky lover Spangle – Ann Beattie invades Updike and Cheever territory to give us a cinematic, brilliantly comic view of America's affluent hell.

'Wonderfully funny' – *The Times*

MOTHER'S HELPER
Maureen Freely

The Pyle-Carpenter household comes complete with three children who can do what they like as long as they have Thought It Through, an intercom that never turns off, with Weekly Family Councils and with the television padlocked into a bag. Like Kay Carpenter herself, it was a totally liberated, principled, caring, warm, nurturing nucleus ... And at first, Laura was completely fooled.

'A novel to weep over or laugh with. Whichever will stop you going mad' – *Literary Review*

DAUGHTERS OF PASSION
Julia O'Faolain

Anger, passion, tenderness, ... nine evocative stories from the author of *No Country for Young Men*. Julia O'Faolain never falters as she moves through situations both strange and familiar – the seduction of a lonely nanny in Paris, a family embarrassed by an unwelcome guest, the sharply focused memories of an imprisoned hunger-striker under pressure to eat. It is a brilliant, compulsive foray into a landscape of passion from a writer at the height of her powers.

LILACS OUT OF THE DEAD LAND
Rachel Billington

April should have been idyllically happy. She and Lawrence have escaped from their jobs and families in England to an illicit holiday in Sicily where – among the beautiful people – they are free to explore uninterrupted passion. But something is wrong. April finds it harder and harder to hold her fragmented life together ... The resulting act of violence shocks and surprises her out of her emotional and sexual captivity.

EVA TROUT
Elizabeth Bowen

'Resonant, beautiful and often very funny ... Eva is triumphantly real, a creation of great imaginative tenderness ... Elizabeth Bowen is a splendid artist, intelligent, generous and acutely aware, who has been telling her readers for many years that love is a necessity, and that its loss or absence is the greatest tragedy man knows' – Julian Jebb in the *Financial Times*

'Rarely have I come across a novel in which sexual frustration (and sexuality) have been so richly and powerfully conveyed' – *Books and Bookmen*

JUDGEMENT DAY
Penelope Lively

Settled into the drowsy village life of Laddenham – where she is playing camp follower to her highly successful husband – clever, agnostic and interested, Clare Paling discovers that small communities offer rivetting sideshows of adultery, gossip and carefully adhered-to pecking orders. It takes the pageant celebrating the church's fourth centenary and an unpardonable death to remind Clare, who had almost forgotten, that the world is a very uncertain place.

'The most enjoyable novel I have read for a very long time indeed' – *The Times*

Some other Penguins by Elizabeth Jane Howard:

GETTING IT RIGHT

Winner of the 1982 *Yorkshire Post* Novel of the Year Award

A hairdresser in the West End, Gavin is sensitive, shy, into the arts, prone to spots and, at thirty-one, a virgin. He's a classic late developer – and maybe it's getting too late to develop at all?

Then one night Gavin finds himself at a posh penthouse party and, caught between Joan and Minerva, suddenly he's developing very rapidly indeed . . . Comedy sparkles, touches and seduces us through the next whirlwind fortnight as Gavin begins, at last, to get it right.

THE SEA CHANGE

Emmanuel is a famous playwright. Lillian is his sickly and embittered wife. They have never quite buried the memory of their dead daughter Sarah. Rich but discontented, they flit from capital to capital with their hero-worshipping young manager – nomads on the international airlines.

Then Alberta, straight from an English vicarage and the pages of Jane Austen, is appointed Emmanuel's secretary. This prim and utterly delightful figure works on the 'family' like milk on a disordered stomach. One by one the leopards change their spots.

THE LONG VIEW

Here is an accurate and revealing portrait of the marriage of Antonia and Conrad Fleming. The ingenious construction of their story offers a remarkable and very real view of the shifting relationship between two people.

'A beautifully written and richly perceptive novel, Miss Howard has a gift for epigrammatic dialogue; she cuts to the heart of motive or relationship with delicate precision' – *Daily Telegraph*

Some other Penguins by Elizabeth Jane Howard:

THE BEAUTIFUL VISIT

On the eve of an unusual voyage, a young woman reviews her life. Her story begins with a 'beautiful visit' to friends in the country which, offering a contrast to the monotony of her home and family, serves as an awakening and an introduction to a new world. What follows is an enchanting and sensitive account of her struggle to retain the mood of her visit and achieve independent happiness.

AFTER JULIUS

It is twenty years since Julius died, but his last heroic action still affects the lives of the people he left behind.

Emma, his youngest daughter, twenty-seven years old and afraid of men.

Cressida, her sister, a war-widow blindly searching for love in her affairs with other women's husbands.

Esme, Julius' widow, still attractive at fifty-eight, but aimlessly lost in the routine of her perfect home.

Felix, Esme's old lover, who left her when Julius died and still feels guilty.

And Dan, an outsider.

Throughout a disastrous – and revelatory – weekend in Sussex, the influence of the dead Julius slowly emerges.

SOMETHING IN DISGUISE

May's second marriage to Colonel Herbert Browne-Lacey is turning out to be a terrible mistake.

Her children find the colonel's presence oppressive and leave home; Oliver to drift from one affair to another, and Elizabeth to follow him to London in search of love and security. Even Herbert's own daughter, the shy and lonely Alice, is driven into marriage to escape from her father's sinister behaviour.

and

ODD GIRL OUT